VIRAGO
MODERN CLASSICS
556

Victoria Mary Sackville-West

Victoria Sackville-West (1892–1962) was born and educated at Knole, the family home that was to be an abiding passion throughout her life. During a brief spell at school in London she met Violet Trefusis with whom she would later have a passionate affair. A distinguished critic, biographer, award-winning poet and gardener, her novels include the acclaimed *All Passion Spent* (1931, dramatised by the BBC in 1986) and *The Edwardians* (1930). Her close friendship with Virginia Woolf is celebrated in Woolf's novel, *Orlando* (1928). In 1930, Vita and her husband Harold Nicolson bought Sissinghurst Castle in Kent, where they created their famous garden. Vita Sackville-West died at home, after an operation for cancer, aged seventy.

Other titles by Victoria Sackville-West include

ALL PASSION SPENT

Vita Sackville-West

Introduced by Joanna Lumley

virago

VIRAGO

Published by Virago Press in 1983
Reprinted 1984, 1986, 1987, 1989, 1990 (twice), 1991 (twice), 1993,
1995, 1996, 1997, 1999, 2000, 2001, 2002, 2003, 2005, 2006, 2007,
2008 (twice), 2009 (twice), 2010

This edition published by Virago Press in 2011
Reprinted 2012 (twice), 2013 (twice)

First published in Great Britain by
The Hogarth Press 1931

A CIP catalogue record for this title
is available from the British Library

ISBN 978-0-86068-358-2

Printed and bound in Great Britain by
Clays Ltd, St Ives plc

Papers used by Virago are from well-managed forests
and other responsible sources.

MIX
Paper from
responsible sources
FSC
www.fsc.org   FSC® C104740

Virago Press
An imprint of
Little, Brown Book Group
100 Victoria Embankment
London EC4Y 0DY

An Hachette UK Company
www.hachette.co.uk

www.virago.co.uk

CONTENTS

CONTENTS

INTRODUCTION

It is always exciting to join a story just as a tumultuous event occurs, in this case the death of a distinguished statesman, Lord Slane, paterfamilias beyond reproach, whose rather ghastly children are themselves already of advanced years, and whose widow ('Mother is wonderful') is widely held to have 'lived only for Father' and to have 'no will of her own'. We have all been there: the hushed voices and changed behaviour of families at death's bedside, trite sentiments veiling underlying anxieties about one's own life being inconvenienced and altered. There is a rustle of expectation about who will be left what, who shall own the jewels, who will benefit from the money, 'the loot', that will have been left. There is the dilemma of who should take responsibility for the bereaved relict, who for the few days between death and funeral is of paramount importance but thereafter becomes an encumbrance.

Although published in 1931, *All Passion Spent* could have been written yesterday, so sharp and relevant are the observations about an old person, in Lady Slane's case eighty-eight years old, who must be cared for as her own days dwindle down. She must be kept safe, and at a convenient distance to visit –

perhaps she should be shunted about regularly so that each of her offspring can help to share the burden. When Lady Slane decides to follow her heart to a house in Hampstead, and live there alone with her devoted and ancient French maid Genoux, it is like a window opening into a different world – a world very shocking to her children. Only Edith, her youngest daughter, thinks her mother 'not mad, but most conspicuously sane'. Edith, the most sympathetic of the tribe, is Lady Slane's favourite child, along with Kay, a strange bachelor figure obsessed with globes, compasses and astrolabes, who cherishes his solitary monkish existence, enlivened by dinners at the club with odd Mr FitzGeorge. The family members are drawn with a keen eye for the absurd, and yet every one is recognisable in our own circle of acquaintances. Sackville-West writes simply wonderfully and many passages make me laugh out loud, for example Lady Slane's first glimpse of Mr Bucktrout as he taps the imaginary barometer on the wall of her new home. Others are utterly beautiful: the butterflies flittering around the carriage as the Slanes travelled through the Persian desert. 'All tiny things, contemptibly tiny things, ennobled only by their vast background, the background of Death.'

As Lady Slane travels to view the property she remembers so well, even though she last saw it thirty years before, she begins her reveries: memories of her past are punctuated by the stations on the Underground, as she passes from the respectable streets of South Kensington into what was then a remote village in north London. The delight that the house inspires in her is infectious; how strange that Vita Sackville-West aged only thirty-eight should have such a clear grasp of an old woman's yearnings. I am halfway between her age when she wrote the book and that of her delicious protagonist, and already I am longing for my own version of her shabby red-brick Georgian house, with its big windows and intruding ivy tendrils, its sunshine and her unexpected and charming companions, Mr Bucktrout, the owner, and Mr Gosheran, the splendid old jack-of-all-trades.

The house is repaired and decorated, and Lady Slane's own life unfolds as she daydreams under the peach tree in the south-facing garden; a character emerges that is very different from the passively serene Vicereine of India known to the outside world. Inside her, waiting to escape but never doing so, is a shy tomboy, a girl who longs to paint, to cut off her hair and dress like a boy, but who somehow stumbles into marriage and hears the door slam forever on her ambitions and hopes. Even though she understands the extent of the sacrifices she will have to make, expectations are such that she feels there is no other choice open to her:

> She supposed that she was not in love with Henry, but, even had she been in love with him, she could see therein no reason for foregoing the whole of her own separate existence. Henry was in love with her, but no one proposed that he should forego his. On the contrary, it appeared that in acquiring her he was merely adding something extra to it ... he would continue to enjoy his free, varied, and masculine life, with no ring upon his finger or difference in his name to indicate the change in his estate; but whenever he felt inclined to come home she must be there ... and even if he beckoned her across the world she must follow ... Her ambitions, her secret existence, all had given way.

Lady Slane becomes 'an appendage' to her husband on marriage, always falling in line with his wishes; a way of life which in her own marriage Vita Sackville-West chose to reject. Vita, in contrast to her fictional heroine, kept her own name, and although she too was married to a diplomat, Harold Nicolson, her writing remained her professional priority. Instead of travelling abroad with her husband on his diplomatic assignments, she chose to remain at home in order to pursue her own career. Eventually Vita persuaded Harold to abandon his diplomatic career entirely so that he was able to stay in England with her. The role of women was a burning issue of the day, and Lady Slane's situation reflects many of the concerns raised in the feminist essay A Room of One's Own, written by Vita's friend and lover Virginia Woolf, and published only two years before.

'She never laid brush to canvas', it is true, but when Lady Slane was discovered arranging flowers on the floor in the vice-regal residency in India, with her small son in a cot beside her, she was engrossed in her painterly placing of colours and shapes (later reflected in Mr Bucktrout's own offerings of flowers in the Hampstead house). Vita Sackville-West's own talents as a gardener seem to fill the pages with a peculiar visual brilliance, as bright as her observations on human behaviour. The revelation that Lady Slane's son's friend, the eccentric and miserly Mr FitzGeorge, was part of her young life comes as a shock, for he too was a different man in those far-off days, when a chance encounter with the beautiful young vicereine as she knelt arranging flowers altered his life forever. He, with a keen collector's eye, loves and amasses things of beauty, but is obsessed by their value; she, like Mr Bucktrout, just loves beauty for itself. He re-enters her life in the most unexpected manner, altering her last months in a way that brings her companionship and a new fortune for her children to worry about.

Events and circumstances are shown as if in a fading photograph in an album, pored over as time ticks by for Lady Slane. A peaceful acceptance of the certainty of death comforts her, and her excellent friend Mr Bucktrout, whose friendship she grows to treasure as much as her visits from Mr FitzGeorge, has philosophies which chime exactly with her own. She loved her husband, but does not miss him, does not miss the splendour of a life that was bounded only by the extent of the British Empire at its peak: horizons begin to shrink as you get older, desires fade away, and belongings become an encumbrance. Her memories parade before her eyes ceaselessly, and become more important than the actual world. By looking back she seems to be searching for an explanation of how her life turned out the way it did, so that she may be reconciled to it before death comes for her.

How marvellous and strange that a book which begins and ends with death should be so joyous and so wickedly funny. This is Vita Sackville-West writing at the height of her powers, and when I finish this introduction I shall pick up the book again and reread it immediately, savouring every sentence, sitting with Lady Slane as the afternoon sunlight slants through the windows into her cosy little drawing room, where she sits, all passion spent, dreaming of days gone by.

Joanna Lumley, 2011

ALL PASSION
SPENT

PART ONE

PART ONE

Henry Lyulph Holland, first Earl of Slane, had existed for so long that the public had begun to regard him as immortal. The public, as a whole, finds reassurance in longevity, and, after the necessary interlude of reaction, is disposed to recognise extreme old age as a sign of excellence. The long-liver has triumphed over at least one of man's initial handicaps: the brevity of life. To filch twenty years from eternal annihilation is to impose one's superiority on an allotted programme. So small is the scale upon which we arrange our values. It was thus with a start of real incredulity that City men, opening their papers in the train on a warm May morning, read that Lord Slane, at the age of ninety-four, had passed away suddenly after dinner on the previous evening. 'Heart failure,' they said sagaciously, though they were actually quoting from the papers; and then added with a sigh, 'Well, another old landmark gone.' That was the dominant feeling: another old landmark gone, another reminder of insecurity. All the events and progressions of Henry Holland's life were gathered up and recorded in a final burst of publicity by the papers; they were gathered together into a handful as hard as a cricket-ball, and flung in the faces of the public, from the days of his 'brilliant university career,' through the days when Mr Holland, at an astonishingly early age, had occupied a seat in the Cabinet, to this very last day when as Earl of Slane, K.G., G.C.B., G.C.S.I., G.C.I.E., etc. etc. – his diminishing honours trailing away behind him like the tail of a comet – he had drooped in his chair after dinner, and the accumulation of ninety years had receded abruptly into history. Time seemed to have made a little jump forward, now that the figure of old Slane was no longer there with outstretched arms to dam it back. For some fifteen years he had taken no very active part in public life, but he had been *there*, and on occasion the irrefutable suavity, common sense, and mockery of his eloquence in Parliament had disturbed, though it could not actually arrest, his more extreme colleagues upon the brink of folly. Such pronouncements had been rare, for Henry Holland had always been a man to appreciate the value of economy, but by their very rarity they produced a wholesome sense of uneasiness, since men knew them to be backed up by a legend of experience: if the old man, the octogenarian, the nonagenarian, could bestir himself to the extent of stalking down to Westminster and unburdening himself, in his incomparable way, of opinions carefully, soberly, but cynically gestated, then the Press and the public were compelled into attention. Nobody had ever seriously attacked Lord Slane. Nobody had ever accused Lord Slane of being a back-number. His humour, his charm, his languor, and his good sense, had rendered him sacrosanct to all generations and to all parties; of him alone among statesmen and politicians, perhaps, could that be said. Perhaps, because he seemed to have touched life on every side, and yet never seemed to have touched life, the common life, at all, by virtue of his proverbial detachment, he had never drawn upon himself the execration and mistrust commonly accorded to the mere expert. Hedonist, humanist, sportsman, philosopher, scholar, charmer, wit; one of those rare Englishmen whose fortune it is to be born equipped with a truly adult mind. His colleagues and his subordinates had been alternately delighted and infuriated by his assumed reluctance to deal with any practical question. It was difficult to get a yes or a no out of the man. The more important a question was, the more flippantly he dealt with it. '*Yes*,' he would write at the bottom of a memorandum setting forth the advantages of two opposite lines of policy; and his myrmidons passed their hands over their brows, distraught. He was destroyed as a statesman, they said, because he always saw both sides of the case; but even as they said it with exasperation, they did not mean it, for they knew that on occasion, when finally pushed into a corner, he would be more incisive, more deadly, than any man seated four-square and full of importance at a governmental desk. He could cast his eye over a report, and pick out its heart and its weakness before another man had had time to read it through. In his exquisitely courteous way, he would annihilate alike the optimism and the myopia of his correspondent. Courteous always, and civilised, he left his competitors dead.

His personal idiosyncrasies, too, were dear to the public as to the caricaturists; his black satin stock, his eyeglass swung on an extravagantly wide ribbon, the coral buttons to his evening waistcoat, the private hansom he maintained long after motors had come into fashion – by all this was he buttressed through the confused justice and injustice of legend; and when, at the age of eighty-five, he finally succeeded in winning the Derby, no man ever received a greater ovation. His wife alone suspected how closely those idiosyncrasies were associated with a settled policy. The least cynical of people by nature, she had learned to lay a veneer of cynicism over herself after seventy years' association with Henry Holland. 'Dear old man,' said the City men in the train; 'well, he's gone.'

He was gone indeed, very finally and irretrievably gone. So thought his widow, looking down at him as he lay on his bed in Elm Park Gardens. The blinds were not lowered, for he had always stipulated that when he came to die the house should not be darkened, and even after his death nobody would have dreamed of disobeying his orders. He lay there in the full sunlight, sparing the stone-mason the trouble of carving his effigy.

His favourite great-grandchild, to whom everything was permitted, had often twitted him, saying that he would make a handsome corpse; and now that the joke had become a reality, the reality gained in impressiveness for having been anticipated by a joke. His was the type of face which, even in life, one associates prophetically with the high dignity of death. The bony architecture of nose, chin, and temples, stood out in greater relief for the slight sinking of the flesh; the lips took a firmer line, and a lifetime of wisdom lay sealed behind them. Moreover, and most importantly, Lord Slane looked as *soigné* in death as he had looked in life. 'Here,' you would say, even though the bedclothes covered him, 'is a dandy.'

Yet, for all its dignity, death brought a revelation. The face which had been so noble in life lost a trifle of its nobility in death; the lips which had been too humorous to be unpleasantly sardonic now betrayed their thinness; the carefully concealed ambition now revealed itself fully in the proud curve of the nostril. The hardness which had disguised itself under the charming manner now remained alone, robbed of the protection of a smile. He was beautiful, but he was less agreeable. Alone in the room his widow contemplated him, filled with thoughts that would greatly have surprised her children, could they but have read her mind.

Her children, however, were not there to observe her. They were collected in the drawing-room, all six of them; two wives and a husband bringing the number up to nine. A sufficiently formidable family gathering – old, black ravens, thought Edith, the youngest, who was always flustered and always trying to confine things into the shape of a phrase, like pouring water into a ewer, but great gouts of meaning and implication invariably ran over and slopped about and were lost. To attempt to recapture them after they had spilt was as hopeless as trying to hold the water in your hand. Perhaps, if one had a notebook and pencil always ready – but then the thought would be lost while one was looking for the right word; and, moreover, it would be difficult to use a notebook without everybody seeing. Shorthand? – but one must not let one's thoughts run on like this; one must discipline one's mind, keeping one's attention on the present matter, as other people seemed to do without any difficulty; though, to be sure, if one had not learnt that lesson by the time one was sixty, one was never likely to learn it. A formidable family gathering, thought Edith, coming back: Herbert, Carrie, Charles, William, and Kay; Mabel, Lavinia; Roland. They went in groups: the Hollands themselves, the sisters-in-law, the brother-in-law; then they sorted themselves differently: Herbert and Mabel, Carrie and Roland; Charles; William and Lavinia; and then Kay all by himself. It was not often that they all met together, none missing – curious, Edith thought, that Death should be the convener, as though all the living rushed instantly together for protection and mutual support. Dear me, how old we all are. Herbert must be sixty-eight, and I'm sixty; and Father was over ninety, and Mother is eighty-eight. Edith, who had begun making a sum of their total ages, surprised them all very much by asking, 'How old are you, Lavinia?' Thus taken aback, they rebuked Edith by their stare; but that was Edith all over, she never listened to what was being said, and then suddenly came out with some irrelevant remark. Edith could have told them that all her life she had been trying to say what she meant, and had never yet succeeded. Only too often, she said something precisely the opposite of what she wanted to say. Her terror was that she should one day use an indecent word by mistake. 'Isn't it splendid that Father is dead,' she might say, instead of, 'Isn't it terrible'; and there were other possibilities, even more appalling, by which one might use a really dreadful word, the sort of word that butcher-boys scrawled in pencil on the white-washed walls of the basement passage, and about which one had to speak, most evasively, to the cook. An unpleasant task; the sort of task that fell to Edith in Elm Park Gardens and to a thousand Ediths all over London. But of these preoccupations her family knew nothing.

They were gratified now to see that she blushed, and that her hands went up nervously to fiddle with the grey strands of her hair; the gesture implied that she had not spoken. Having reduced her to this confusion, they returned to their conversation, suitably hushed and mournful. Even the voices of Herbert and Carrie, habitually insistent, were lowered. Their father lay upstairs, and their mother was with him.

'Mother is wonderful.'

Over and over, thought Edith, they had reiterated that phrase. Surprise was in their accents, as though they had expected their mother to rant, rave, scream, give herself up for lost. Edith knew very well that her brothers and sister privately entertained a theory that their mother was rather a simpleton. From time to time she let fall remarks that could not be reconciled with ordinary sense; she had no grasp on the world as it was; she was apt to say impetuous things which, although uttered in English, made no more sense than had they been uttered in an outer-planetary language. Mother was a changeling, they had often said politely, in the bitter-sweet accents reserved for a family joke; but now in this emergency they found a new phrase: Mother is wonderful. It was the thing they were expected to say, so they said it, several times over, like a refrain coming periodically into their conversation and sweeping it upwards on to a higher level. Then it drooped again; became practical. Mother was wonderful, but what was to be done with Mother? Evidently, she could not go on being wonderful for the rest of her life. Somewhere, somehow, she must be allowed to break down, and then, after that was over, must be stowed away; housed, taken care of. Outside, in the streets, the posters might flare: DEATH OF LORD SLANE. The journalists might run up and down Fleet Street assembling their copy; they might pounce on the pigeon-holes – that macabre columbarium – where the obituary notices were stored in readiness; they might raid each other's information: 'I say, is it true that old Slane always carried his cash in coppers? wore crêpe soles? dipped his bread in his coffee?' Anything to make a good paragraph. Telegraph-boys might ring the bell, propping their red bicycles against the kerb, delivering their brown messages of condolence, from all over the world, from all parts of the Empire, especially where Lord Slane had served his term of government. Florists might deliver their wreaths – already the narrow hall was full of them – 'indecently soon,' said Herbert, peering jealously nevertheless at the attached cards through his monocle. Old friends might call – 'Herbert – so dreadfully sudden – of course, I didn't expect to see your dear Mother—' But obviously they had expected it, had expected to be the sole exception, and Herbert must turn them away, rather enjoying it: 'Mother, you understand, is naturally rather overcome; wonderful, I must say; but just at present, you'll understand, I'm sure, is seeing nobody but Us'; and so with many pressings of Herbert's hand they took their departure, having got no further than the hall or the doorstep. Reporters might loiter on the pavement, dangling cameras like black concertinas. All this might go on outside the house, but inside it, upstairs, Mother was with Father and the problem of her future lay heavy upon her sons and daughters.

Of course, she would not question the wisdom of any arrangements they might choose to make. Mother had no will of her own; all her life long, gracious and gentle, she had been wholly submissive – an appendage. It was assumed that she had not enough brain to be self-assertive. 'Thank goodness,' Herbert sometimes remarked, 'Mother is not one of those clever women.' That she might have ideas which she kept to herself never entered into their estimate. They anticipated no trouble with their mother. That she might turn round and play a trick on them – several tricks – after years of being merely a fluttering lovable presence amongst them, never entered into their calculations either. She was not a clever woman. She would be grateful to them for arranging her few remaining years.

They stood in the drawing-room in a group, uncomfortably shifting from one foot to the other, but it never occurred to them to sit down. They would have thought it disrespectful. For all their good solid sense, death, even an expected death, disconcerted them just a little. Around them hung that uneasy, unsettled air which attends those about to set out on a journey or those whose lives have been seriously disturbed. Edith would have liked to sit down, but dared not. How large they all were, she thought; large and black and elderly, with grandchildren of their own. How lucky, she thought, that we all wear so much black habitually, for we certainly could not have got our mourning yet, and how terrible it would have been for Carrie to arrive in a pink shirt. As it was, they were all black as crows, and Carrie's black gloves lay on the writing-table with her boa and her bag. The ladies of the Holland family still wore boas, high collars, and long skirts which they had to hold up when they crossed the road; any concession to fashion was, they felt, unbecoming to their age. Edith admired her sister Carrie. She did not love her, and she was frightened of her, but she admired and envied her tremendously. Carrie had inherited her father's eagle nose and commanding presence; she was tall, pale, and distinguished. Herbert, Charles, and William were tall and distinguished also; only Kay and Edith were dumpy. Edith's thoughts were straying again: we might belong to a different family, she thought, Kay and I. Kay in fact was a chubby little old gentleman, with bright blue eyes and a neat white beard;

12

there, again, he differed from his brothers who were clean-shaven. What a queer thing appearance was, and how unfair. It dictated the terms of people's estimate throughout one's whole life. If one looked insignificant, one was set down as insignificant; yet, one probably didn't look insignificant unless one deserved it. But Kay seemed quite happy; he didn't worry about significance, or about anything else; his bachelor rooms, and his collection of compasses and astrolabes seemed to satisfy him quite as well as public esteem, or a wife and a more personal life. For he was the greatest living authority upon globes, compasses, astrolabes, and all kindred instruments; lucky Kay, thought Edith, to have concentrated so contentedly upon one little department. (Curious symbols to have chosen, though, for one who had never loved the sea or climbed a mountain; to him, they were collector's pieces, ranged and ticketed, but to Edith, the romantic, a vast dark world rose beyond their small brass and mahogany, their intricacy of pivots and gimbals, discs and circles, the guinea-gold brass and the nut-brown wood, the signs of the Zodiac and the dolphins spouting up the ocean; a vast dark world where nothing was charted on the maps but regions of danger and uncertainty, and ragged men chewed bullets to allay their thirst.) 'Then there is the question of income,' William was saying.

How characteristic of William to mix up Mother's future with questions of income; for to William and Lavinia parsimony was in itself a career. An apple bruised by falling prematurely from the tree must immediately be turned into a dumpling lest it be wasted. Waste was the bugbear of William's and Lavinia's life. The very newspaper must be rolled into spills to save the matches. They had a passion for getting something for nothing. Every blackberry in the hedgerow was an agony to Lavinia until she had bottled it. Living, as they did, at Godalming with two acres of ground, they spent painful-happy evenings in calculation as to whether a pig could be made to pay on the household scraps, and whether a dozen hens could out-balance their corn in eggs. Well, thought Edith, they must pass the time very absorbingly with such a constant preoccupation; but how miserable it must make them to think of all the sacks of gold squandered by them since their marriage. Let me see, thought Edith, William is the fourth, so he must be sixty-four; he must have been married for thirty years, so if they have spent fifteen hundred a year – what with the children's education and all – that makes forty-five thousand pounds; sacks and sacks of treasure, such as the divers are always looking for at Tobermory. But Herbert was saying something. Herbert was always full of information; and the surprising thing was, for such a stupid man, it was usually correct.

'I can tell you all about that.' He put two fingers inside his collar, adjusted it, jerking his chin upward, cleared his throat, and gave a preliminary glare at his relations. 'I can tell you all about that. I discussed it with Father – he took me, I may say, into his confidence. Ahem! Father, as you know, was not a rich man, and most of his income dies with him. Mother will be left with a net income of five hundred a year.'

They digested this fact. William and Lavinia exchanged glances, and it could be seen that their minds were involved in rapid and experienced calculations. Edith, who passed privately among her relations for a half-wit, could on occasions be surprisingly shrewd – she had a habit of seeing through people's words right down into their motives, and of stating her deductions with a frankness that was disconcerting rather than discreet. She knew now quite well what William was about to say, though for once she held her tongue. But she chuckled to herself as she heard him say it.

'I suppose Father didn't happen to mention the jewels in the course of his confidences, did he, Herbert?'

'He did. The jewels, as you know, form not the least valuable part of his estate. They were his private property, and he has seen fit to leave them unconditionally to Mother.'

That's a smack for Herbert and Mabel, thought Edith. I suppose they expected Father to leave the jewels, like heirlooms, to his eldest son. A glance at Mabel's face showed her, however, that the announcement came as no surprise. Evidently Herbert had already repeated his father's confidences to his wife – and Mabel had been lucky, thought Edith, if Herbert had betrayed no irritation against her for thus failing to turn him into a successful legatee.

'In that case,' said William decisively – for although he and Lavinia had hoped for a portion of the jewels, it was pleasing to think that Herbert and Mabel also had been disappointed – 'in that case Mother will certainly wish to sell them. And quite right too. Why should she keep a lot of useless jewellery lying in the bank? In my opinion the jewels should fetch from five to seven thousand pounds, properly handled.'

'But more important than the question of jewels or income,' Herbert proceeded, 'is the question of where Mother is to live. She cannot be left alone. In any case, she could not afford to keep on this house. It must be sold. Where, then, is she to go?' Another glare. 'Clearly, it is our duty to look after her. She must make her home among us.' It was like a set speech.

All these old people, thought Edith, disposing of a still older person! Still, it seemed inevitable. Mother would parcel out her year: three months with Herbert and Mabel, three with Carrie and Roland, three with Charles, three with William and Lavinia – then where did she herself and Kay come in? Rising once more to the surface of her reflections, she launched one of her sudden and ill-chosen remarks, 'But surely I ought to bear the brunt – I've always lived at home – I'm unmarried.'

'Brunt?' said Carrie, turning on her. Edith was instantly annihilated. 'Brunt? My dear Edith! Who spoke of brunt? I'm sure we shall all regard it as a joy – a privilege – to do our part in looking after Mother in these last sad years of her life – for sad they must be, deprived of the one thing she lived for. Brunt, I think, is scarcely the word, Edith.'

Edith subserviently agreed: it wasn't. Spoken like that, repeated several times over, without the support of its usual little phrase, it acquired a strange and uncouth semblance, like spick without span, hoity without toity, turvy without topsy. It became a rude and Saxon word, like woad, or witenagemot; brunt, blunt; a blunt word. And what did it mean, to bear the brunt? What was a brunt, anyhow? No, brunt was not the word. 'Well,' said Edith, 'I think I ought to live with Mother.'

She saw relief spread itself over Kay's face; he had been thinking, that was evident, of his snug little rooms and his collection. Herbert's voice had been as a trumpet threatening the walls of his Jericho. The others, also, considered Edith and the possibility she offered them. The unmarried daughter; she was the obvious solution. But the Hollands were not people to evade a duty, and the more irksome the duty, the less likely were they to evade it. Joy was a matter they seldom considered, but duty was ever present with them, seriously always and sometimes grimly. Their father's energy had passed on to them, turning a trifle sour on the way. Carrie spoke up for her relations. Carrie was good; but, like so many good people, she always managed to set everybody by the ears.

'There is certainly something in what Edith says. She has always lived at home, and the change would not be very great for her. I know, of course, that she has often wished for independence and a home of her own; dear Edith,' she said, with a digressive smile; 'but quite rightly, as I think,' she continued,

16

'she refused to leave Father and Mother so long as she could be of use to them. I feel now, however, that we ought all to take our share. We must not take advantage of Edith's unselfishness, or of Mother's. I am sure I speak for you too, Herbert, and for you, William. It would be greatly to Mother's benefit if, instead of embarking on a new house, she could make her home amongst us all in turn.'

'Quite so,' said Herbert approving, and again adjusting his collar; 'quite so, quite so.'

William and Lavinia again exchanged glances.

'Of course,' William began, 'in spite of our limited income Lavinia and I would always be happy to welcome Mother. At the same time I think some financial arrangement should be come to. So much more satisfactory for Mother. She would then feel no embarrassment. Two pounds a week, perhaps, or thirty-five shillings . . .'

'I entirely agree with William,' said Charles unexpectedly; 'speaking for myself, a general's pension is so absurdly inadequate that I should find an additional guest a serious drain on my resources. As you know, I live very modestly in a small flat. I have no spare bedroom. Of course, I have hopes that the question of pensions may some day be adjusted. I have written a long memorandum to the War Office about it, also a letter to *The Times*, which no doubt they are holding in reserve until a suitable occasion, as they have not yet printed it, though, I confess, I see very little hope of reform under this present miserable Government.' Charles snorted. He felt that that was rather a good speech, and looked round at his family for approval. He was not General Sir Charles Holland for nothing.

'Isn't it rather delicate . . .' began the new Lady Slane.

'Be quiet, Mabel,' said Herbert. He was seldom known to address any other phrase to his wife, nor did Mabel often succeed in getting beyond her four or five opening words. 'This is entirely a family matter, please. In any case, it cannot be discussed in any detail until after – h'm – poor Father's funeral. I do not quite know how this unpleasant subject has arisen. (That's one for William, thought Edith.) In the meantime Mother must, of course, be our first consideration. Anything which can be done to spare her feelings … After all, we must remember that her life is shattered. You know that she lived only for Father. And we should be very seriously and rightly blamed if we were to abandon her now to her loneliness.'

Ah, that's it, thought Edith: what will people say? So they mean to combine people's good opinion with getting a little of poor Mother's money. Wrangle, wrangle, she thought – for she had had some previous taste of family discussions; they'll wrangle for weeks over Mother like dogs quarrelling over an old, a very old, bone. Only Kay will try to keep out of it. William and Lavinia will be the worst; they'll want to get Mother as a paying guest, and then look down their noses while their friends praise them. And Carrie will wear an air of high martyrdom. This is the sort of thing, she thought, which happens when people die. Then she discovered that underneath this current of thought was running another current, concerned with whether she would now be able to live independently; she saw the little flat which would be her own; the cheerful sitting-room; the one servant, and the latchkey; the evenings over the fire with a book. No more answering letters for Father; no more accompanying Mother when she went to open hospital wards; no more adding up the house-books; no more taking Father for a walk in the Park. And at last she would be able to have a canary. How could she help hoping that Herbert, Carrie, Charles, and William would divide Mother between them? Shocked though she was by their blatancy, she acknowledged inwardly that she was no better than the rest of her family.

*

18

Edith was frightened of being left in this strange house, alone with her living mother and her dead father. She could not own to her fear, but she did everything in her power to delay the departure of her brothers and sister. Even Carrie and Herbert, whom she rather disliked, and Charles and William, whom she rather despised, became desirable to her as presences and companions. She invented pretexts to keep them back, dreading the moment when the front door would shut finally behind them. Even Kay would have been better than nothing. But Kay slipped from her before the others. She fluttered after him on to the landing; he turned to see who was following him; turned, with his neat little white beard and his comfortable little paunch, crossed by a watch-chain. 'You're going, Kay?' He was annoyed, because he imagined a reproof in Edith's tone, where, really, he should have detected only an appeal. He was annoyed, because he already had a sense of guilt in his intention of keeping an engagement; ought he, rather, to have remained to dinner at Elm Park Gardens? Then he had consoled his conscience by reflecting that the servants must not be given any extra trouble. So, when Edith ran after him, he turned, looking as patiently annoyed as it was possible for him to look. 'You're going, Kay?'

Kay was going. He must get some dinner. He could come back later, if Edith thought it desirable. He added this, being cowardly though self-indulgent, and anxious to avoid unpleasantness at any cost. Fortunately for him, Edith was cowardly too, and immediately retracted any reproof or appeal her pursuit might have been intended to convey. 'Oh no, Kay, of course not; why should you come back? I'll look after Mother. You'll be coming in to-morrow morning?'

Yes, said Kay, relieved; he'd come in to-morrow morning. Early. They kissed. They had not kissed for many years; but that was one of the strange effects of death: elderly brothers and sisters pecked at one another's cheeks. Their noses, from lack of custom, got in the way. Both of them looked up the dark well of the staircase, after they had kissed, towards the floor where their father lay, and then in sudden embarrassment Kay scuttled off down the stairs. He felt a relief as he shut himself out into the street. A May evening; normal London; taxis passing in the King's Road; and FitzGeorge waiting for him at the club. He must not keep Fitz waiting. He would not go by bus. He would take a taxi.

FitzGeorge was his oldest, indeed his only, friend. Over twenty years of difference in age separated them, but after threescore such discrepancies begin to close up. The two old gentlemen had many tastes in common. They were both ardent collectors, the only difference between them being a difference of wealth. FitzGeorge was enormously rich; a millionaire. Kay Holland was poor – all the Hollands were comparatively poor, although their father had been Viceroy of India. FitzGeorge could buy anything he liked, but such was his eccentricity that he lived like a pauper in two rooms at the top of a house in Bernard Street, and took pleasure in a work of art only if it had been his own discovery and a bargain. Since he possessed an extraordinary instinct for discoveries and bargains – finding unsuspected Donatellos in the basement of large furniture shops in the Tottenham Court Road – he had amassed at small cost (to his own delight and to Kay Holland's envious but exasperated admiration) a miscellaneous collection coveted by the British and the South Kensington Museums alike. Nobody knew what he would do with his things. He was just as likely to bequeath them all to Kay Holland as to make a bonfire of them in Russell Square. Obvious heirs he had none, any more than he had obvious progenitors. Meanwhile he kept his treasures closely round him; the few people privileged to visit him in his two rooms came away with a tale of Ming figures rolled up in a pair of socks, Leonardo drawings stacked in the bath, Elamite pottery ranged upon the chairs. Certainly, during the visit one had to remain standing, for there was no free chair to sit on; and jade bowls must be cleared away before Mr FitzGeorge could grudgingly offer one a cup of the cheapest tea, boiling the kettle himself on a gas-ring. The only visitors to receive a second invitation were those who had declined the tea.

Nearly everybody knew him by sight. When people saw his square hat and old-fashioned frock-coat going into Christie's they said, 'There's old Fitz.' Winter or summer, his costume never varied; square hat, frock-coat, and usually a parcel carried under his arm. What the parcel contained was never divulged; it might be a Dresden cup, or a kipper for Mr FitzGeorge's supper. Londoners felt affectionately towards him, as one of their genuine eccentrics, but no one, not even Kay Holland, would have dreamed of calling him Fitz to his face, however glibly they might say 'There's old Fitz' when they saw him pass. It was said that the happiest event of his life was the death of Lord Clanricarde; on that day, old Fitz had walked down St James's Street with a flower in his buttonhole, and all the other gentlemen sitting in club windows had known perfectly well why.

Although Mr FitzGeorge and Kay Holland had been friends for some thirty years, no personal intimacy existed between them. When they sat at dinner together – a familiar spectacle in Boodle's or the Thatched House Club, each paying his share, and drinking barley-water – they discussed prices and catalogues as inexhaustibly as lovers discuss their emotions, but beyond this they knew nothing of each other whatsoever. Mr FitzGeorge knew, of course, that Kay was old Slane's son, but Kay knew no more of Mr FitzGeorge's parentage than anybody else. Quite possibly Mr FitzGeorge himself knew nothing of it either; so people said, basing their suspicions on the suggestive prefix to his name. Certainly Kay had never asked him; had never even hinted at any curiosity on the subject. Their relationship was beautifully detached. This explains why Mr FitzGeorge awaited Kay's arrival in some perturbation, uncomfortably aware that he ought to make some allusion to the Hollands' bereavement, but shrinking from this infringement of their tacit understanding. He felt vexed with Kay; it was inconsiderate of him to have lost his father, inconsiderate of him not to have cancelled their appointment; yet Mr FitzGeorge knew quite well that a cancelled appointment was a crime he never forgave. Very cross, he watched for Kay's approach, drumming on the window at Boodle's. He must say something, he supposed; better to do it at once, and get it over. Surely Kay was not going to be late? He had never yet been late for an appointment, in thirty years; never been late, and never failed to turn up. Mr FitzGeorge drew an enormous silver turnip, price five shillings, from his pocket and looked at the time. Seventeen minutes past eight. He compared it with the clock on St James's Palace. Kay was late; two whole minutes. – But there he was, getting out of a taxi.

'Evening,' said Kay, coming into the room.

'Evening,' said Mr FitzGeorge. 'You're late.'

'Dear me, so I am,' said Kay. 'Let us go in to dinner at once, shall we?'

During dinner they talked about a pair of Sèvres bowls which Mr FitzGeorge alleged that he had discovered in the Fulham Road. Kay, who had seen them too, was of the opinion that they were fakes, and this divergence led to one of those discussions which both old gentlemen so thoroughly enjoyed. But this evening, Mr FitzGeorge's pleasure was spoilt; he had not said what he intended to say, and every moment made the saying of it more awkward and more impossible. His irritation against Kay was increased. It was the first unsuccessful meal that they

22

had ever had together, and the disappointment made Mr Fitz-George reflect that all friendship was a mistake; he regretted crossly that he had ever allowed himself to become involved with Kay; other people had always been kept at arm's length, a most commendable system; it was a mistake, a great mistake, to admit exceptions. He scowled across the table at Kay, drinking his barley-water and carefully wiping his neat little beard, unaware of the hostility he was arousing.

'Coffee?' said Mr FitzGeorge.

'I think so – yes, coffee.'

Poor old chap, he looks tired, thought Mr FitzGeorge suddenly; not quite so spruce as usual; he's drooping a little; he's been making an effort to talk. 'Have a brandy?' he said.

Kay looked up, surprised. They never had brandy.

'No, thanks.'

'Yes. Waiter, give Mr Holland a brandy. Put it down on my bill.'

'I really . . .' began Kay.

'Nonsense. Waiter, the best brandy – the eighteen forty. When all's said and done, Holland, I saw you in your cradle. The eighteen forty brandy was only thirty years old or so then. So don't make a fuss.'

Kay made no fuss, startled as he was by this sudden revelation that old Fitz had seen him in his cradle. His mind flung itself back wildly into time and space. Time: 1874; space: India. So old Fitz must have been in India in 1874. 'You never told me that you had been in Calcutta then,' said Kay, sipping his brandy over his little Vandyck beard. 'Didn't I?' said old Fitz negligently, as though it were of no importance; 'well, I was. My guardians didn't approve of universities, and sent me round the world instead. (Strange revelations! so old Fitz, in his adolescence, had been controlled by guardians?) Your parents were very kind to me,' Mr FitzGeorge proceeded; 'naturally, your father as Viceroy hadn't much leisure, but your mother, I remember, was most gracious; most charming. She was young then; young, and very lovely. I remember thinking that she was the most lovely thing I had seen in India. – But you're wrong about those bowls all the same, Holland. You know nothing whatever about china – never did, never will. It's too fine a taste for you. You ought to confine yourself to junk like your astrolabes. That's all you're fit for. Setting yourself up as a judge of china, indeed! And against me, who have forgotten more about china than you ever learnt.'

Kay was well accustomed to such abuse; he liked being bullied by old Fitz; it gave him a little tremor of delight. He sat listening while old Fitz told him that he did not deserve the name of connoisseur, and would have done much better to go in for collecting stamps. He knew that Fitz did not mean a word of it, but enjoyed pecking at him like an old, pecking, courting pigeon, while Kay averted his head and dodged the blows, laughing a little meanwhile, ever so slightly arch, and looking down at the table-cloth, fingering the knives and forks. Their relations had miraculously got back to the normal, and so greatly did Mr FitzGeorge's spirits rise at this re-establishment that he said presently he was dashed if he wouldn't have a brandy too. He had forgotten all about that difficult allusion he intended to make, or thought he had forgotten, but perhaps it had really been in his mind all the time, for when they came out of the club together, and stood on the steps preparing to part, while Kay pulled on his chamois-leather gloves – Mr FitzGeorge had never owned a pair of gloves in his life, but Kay Holland was never seen without his hands gloved in butter-yellow – to his own surprise he heard himself growl out, 'Sorry to hear about your father, Holland.'

There, it was said, and St James's Street had not opened to swallow him up. It was said; it had been quite easy, really. But what on earth was prompting him to go further to make the most incredible, unnecessary proposal? – 'Perhaps some day you'll take me to call on Lady Slane.' Now what had possessed him to say that? Kay looked taken aback; and no wonder. 'Oh, yes – yes, certainly – if you'd care to come,' he said hurriedly. 'Well, good-night – good-night,' and he hurried away, while old Fitz stood staring after him, wondering whether he had made it impossible for himself ever to see Kay Holland again.

The house was strange – thus Edith pursued her thoughts – there was such a contrast between what went on inside and what went on outside. Outside it was all blare and glare and publicity, what with the posters, and the reporters still hanging about the area railings, and the talk of Westminster Abbey, and speeches in both Houses of Parliament. Inside it was all hushed and private, like a conspiracy; the servants whispered, people went soundlessly up and down stairs; and whenever Lady Slane came into the room everybody stopped talking, and stood up, and somebody was sure to go forward and lead her gently to a chair. They treated her rather as though she had had an accident, or had gone temporarily off her head. Yet Edith was sure her mother did not want to be led to chairs, or to be kissed so reverently and mutely, or to be asked if she was sure she wouldn't rather have dinner in her room. The only person to treat her in a normal way was Genoux, her old French maid, who was nearly as old as Lady Slane herself, and had been with her for the whole of her married life. Genoux moved about the house as noisily as ever, talking to herself as her custom was, muttering to herself about her next business in her extraordinary jumble of French and English; she still burst unceremoniously into the drawing-room in pursuit of her mistress, whoever might be there, and horrified the assembled family by asking, 'Pardon, miladi, est-ce que ça vaut la peine d'envoyer les shirts de milord à la wash?'

They all looked at Lady Slane as though they expected her to fall instantly to pieces, like a vase after a blow, but she replied in her usual quiet voice that yes, his lordship's shirts must certainly be sent to the wash; and then, turning to Herbert, said, 'I don't know what you would like me to do with your father's things, Herbert; it seems a pity to give them all to the butler, and anyway they wouldn't fit.'

Her mother and Genoux, Edith thought, alone refused to adapt themselves to the strangeness of the house. She could read disapproval in the eyes of Herbert, Carrie, Charles, and William; but naturally no disapproval could be openly expressed. They could only insist, implicitly, that their own convention must be adopted: Mother's life was shattered, Mother was bearing up wonderfully, Mother must be sheltered within the privacy of her disaster, while the necessary business was conducted, the necessary contact with the outside world maintained, by her capable sons and her capable daughter. Edith, poor thing, wasn't much use. Everybody knew that Edith always said the wrong thing at the wrong moment, and left undone everything that she was supposed to do, giving as her excuse that she had been 'too busy'; nor was Kay of much use either, but then he scarcely counted as a member of the family at all. Herbert, Carrie, William, and Charles stood between their mother and the outside world. From time to time, indeed, some special rumour was allowed to creep past their barrier: the King and Queen had sent a most affectionate message – Herbert could scarcely be expected to keep that piece of news to himself. Huddersfield, Lord Slane's native town, desired the approval of the family for a memorial service. The King would be represented at the funeral by the Duke of Gloucester. The ladies of the Royal School of Embroidery had worked – in a great hurry – a pall. The Prime Minister would carry one corner of it; the Leader of the Opposition another. The French Government were sending a representative; and it was said that the Duke of Brabant might attend on behalf of the Belgian. These bits of information were imparted to his mother by Herbert in driblets and with caution; he was feeling his way to see how she would receive them. She received them with complete indifference. 'Very nice of them, to be sure,' she said; and once she said, 'So glad, dear, if you're pleased.' Herbert both relished and resented this remark. Any tribute paid to his father was paid to himself, in a way, as head of the family; yet his mother's place, rightfully, was in the centre of the picture; these three or four days between death and burial were, rightfully, her own. Herbert prided himself on his sense of fitness. Plenty of time, afterwards, to assert himself as Lord Slane. Generation must tread upon the heels of generation – that was a law of nature; yet, so long as his father's physical presence remained in the house, his mother had the right to authority. By her indifference, she was abdicating her position unnecessarily, unbecomingly, soon. She ought, posthumously, for these three or four days, to rally supremely in honour of her husband's memory; any abrogation of her right was unseemly. So it ran in Herbert's code. But perhaps, chattered the imp in Edith, perhaps she was so thoroughly drained by Father in his lifetime that she can't now be bothered with his memory?

Certainly the house was strange, with a particular strangeness that had never invaded it before and could never invade it again. Father could not die twice. By his dying he had created this particular situation – a situation which, surely, he had never foreseen; the sort of situation which nobody would foresee until it came actually into being. Nobody could have foreseen that Father, so dominant always, so paramount, would by the mere act of dying turn Mother into the most prominent figure. Her prominence might last only for three or four days; but during that brief spell it must be absolute. Everybody must defer. She, and she alone, must decide whether the doors of Westminster

27

Abbey should or should not revolve upon their hinges; a nation must wait upon her decision, a Dean and Chapter truckle to her wishes. Very gently, and cautiously, she must be consulted on every point, and her views ascertained. It was very strange that somebody so self-eclipsing should suddenly have turned into somebody so important. It was like playing a game; it reminded Edith of the days when Father in one of his gay moods would come into the drawing-room after tea to find Mother with all the children around her, reading to them perhaps out of a storybook, and would clap the book shut and say that now they would all play follow-my-leader all through the house, but that Mother must lead. So they had gone, capering through silent chanceries and over the parquet floors of ballrooms, where the chandeliers hung in their holland bags, performing all kinds of absurd antics on the way – for Mother had an inexhaustible invention – and Father would follow last, bringing up the tail, but always playing the clown and getting all his imitations wrong, whereat the children would shriek with delight, pretending to put him right, and Mother would turn round with Kay clinging on to her skirts, to say with assumed severity, 'Really, Henry!' Many an Embassy and Government House had rung to their evening laughter. But once, Edith remembered, Mother (who was young then) had tumbled some papers in the archivist's room out of a file, and, as the children had scrambled joyfully to make the disorder worse, Father had darkened suddenly, he had conveyed displeasure in a grown-up way; his gaiety and Mother's had collapsed together like a rose falling to pieces; and the return to the drawing-room had been made in a sort of scolded silence, as though Jove stooping from Olympus had detected a mortal taking liberties in his pretended absence with his high concerns.

But now Mother might play follow-my-leader as she would; for three or four days Mother might play follow-my-leader, leading the dignitaries of Europe and of Empire some dance up to Golder's Green or Huddersfield as the fancy took her, instead of resigning herself to Westminster Abbey or Brompton Cemetery as was expected; but the disappointment – to the imp in Edith's mind – lay in Mother's refusal to take any lead at all. She simply agreed to everything that Herbert suggested. Just as well might Herbert, at the age of seven, playing follow-my-leader, have prompted her, 'Now let's romp through the kitchens;' her acquiescence to-day, when she was eighty-eight and Herbert sixty-eight, shocked Edith as something unfitting. It shocked Herbert too – though, true son of his father, he was flattered by womanly dependence. Only for these three or four days – since he was playing a game, subscribing to a convention – did he demand of his mother that she should hold opinions of her own. Yet at the same time, such was his masculine contrariness, he would have resented any decision running counter to his own ideas.

Herbert, then, became gentler and gentler as he saw his own ideas adopted and yet could persuade himself that they had originated with his mother and not with him. He came down from his mother's room to his brothers and sisters, again – continuously, as it seemed to Edith – assembled in the drawing-room. Mother wanted the Abbey; therefore the Abbey it must be. After all, Mother was doubtless right. All England's greatest sons were buried in the Abbey. He himself would have preferred the parish church at Huddersfield, he said, though Edith shrewdly estimated the honesty of this remark, and in speaking for himself he thought he might speak for them all; but Mother's wishes must be considered. They must bow to the publicity of the Abbey. After all, it was an honour – a great honour – the crowning honour of their father's life. Carrie, William, and Charles inclined their heads in silence at this solemn thought. Edith, on the other hand, thought how much amused her father would have been, and at the same time how much gratified, though professing scornfulness, could he have watched himself being buried in the Abbey.

The pall worked by the ladies of the Royal School of Embroidery was undoubtedly very sumptuous. Heraldic emblems were embossed on violet plush. The Prime Minister duly carried his corner, becomingly serious, and so satisfactorily in character that no one seeing him could have hesitated to say, 'There goes a Prime, or at any rate a Cabinet, Minister of England.' The Leader of the Opposition kept step with the Prime Minister; for an hour they had buried their differences, which, indeed, were part of a game too, since under the tuition of a common responsibility they had both absorbed much the same lessons, though their adherents forbade them to repeat them in the same language. The two young princes, ushered hurriedly though respectfully to their seats, wondered, perhaps, why fate had isolated them from other young men, by condemning them to cut tapes across new arterial roads or to honour statesmen by attending their funerals. More probably, they took it all as part of the day's work.

But where, meanwhile, Edith wondered, was reality?

After the funeral was over, everything at Elm Park Gardens subtly changed. Consideration towards Lady Slane was still observed, but a note of impatience crept in, a note of domination, held rather insistently by Herbert and Carrie. Herbert had become, quite definitely, the head of the family, and Carrie his support. They were prepared to take a firm though kind line with their mother. She could still be led to a chair, and, once lowered into it, could still be patted on the shoulder with a kindly protective gesture, but she must be made to understand that the affairs of the world were waiting, and that this pause of concession to death could not go on for ever. Like the papers in Lord Slane's desk, Lady Slane must be cleared up; then Herbert and Carrie could get back to their business.

Nothing not put actually into words could have been conveyed more plainly.

Very quiet, very distinguished, very old, very frail, Lady Slane sat looking at her sons and daughters. Her children, who were accustomed to her, took her appearance for granted, but strangers exclaimed in amazement that she could not be over seventy. She was a beautiful old woman. Tall, slender, and pale, she had never lost her grace or her carriage. Clothes upon her ceased to be clothes and became draperies; she had the secret of line. A fluid loveliness ran over all her limbs. Her eyes were grey and deeply set; her nose was short and straight; her tranquil hands the hands of a Vandyck; over her white hair fell a veil of black lace, highly becoming. Her gowns for years past had always been soft, indefinite, and of unrelieved black. Looking at her, one could believe that it was easy for a woman to be beautiful and gracious, as all works of genius persuade us that they were effortless of achievement. It was more difficult to believe in the activity that Lady Slane had learned to pack into her life. Duty, charity, children, social obligations, public appearances – with these had her days been filled; and whenever her name was mentioned, the corollary came quick and slick, 'Such a wonderful help to her husband in his career!' Oh yes, thought Edith, Mother is lovely; Mother, as Herbert says, is wonderful. But Herbert is clearing his throat. What's coming now?

'Mother, dear ...' A form of address semi-childish, semi-conventional; Herbert putting his fingers into his collar. Yet she had once sat on the floor beside him, and shown him how to spin his top.

'Mother, dear. We have been discussing ... we have, I mean, felt naturally troubled about your future. We know how devoted you were to Father, and we realise the blank that his loss must leave in your life. We have been wondering – and that is why

31

we have asked you to meet us all here in the drawing-room before we separate again to our different homes – we have been wondering where and how you will choose to live?'

'But you have decided it already for me, Herbert, haven't you?' said Lady Slane with the utmost sweetness.

Herbert put his fingers into his collar and peeked and preened until Edith feared that he would choke.

'Well! decided it for you, Mother, dear! decided is scarcely the word. It is true that we have sketched out a little scheme, which we could submit for your approval. We have taken your tastes into consideration, and we have realised that you would not like to be parted from so many interests and occupations. At the same time ...'

'One moment, Herbert,' said Lady Slane; 'what was that you said about interests and occupations?'

'Surely, Mother, dear,' said Carrie reproachfully, 'Herbert means all your committees, the Battersea Club for Poor Women, the Foundlings' Ward, the Unfortunate Sisters' Organisation, the ...'

'Oh yes,' said Lady Slane; 'my interests and occupations. Quite. Go on, Herbert.'

'All these things,' said Carrie, 'would collapse without you. We realise that. You founded many of them. You have been the life of others. Naturally, you won't want to abandon them now.'

'Besides, dear Lady Slane,' said Lavinia – she had never unbent sufficiently to address her mother-in-law by any other name – 'we realise how bored you would be with nothing to do. You so active, so energetic! Oh no, we couldn't visualise you anywhere but in London.'

Still Lady Slane said nothing. She looked from one to the other with an expression that, in one so gentle, was surprisingly ironical.

'At the same time,' Herbert proceeded, reverting to his original speech whose interruption he had endured, patient though not pleased, 'your income will scarcely suffice for the expenses of a house such as you are entitled to expect. We propose, therefore ...' and he outlined the scheme which we have already heard discussed, and may consequently spare ourselves the trouble of listening to again.

Lady Slane, however, listened. She had spent a great deal of her life listening, without making much comment, and now she listened to her eldest son without making any comment at all. He, for his part, was unperturbed by her silence. He knew that all her life she had been accustomed to have her comings and goings and stayings arranged for her, whether she was told to board a steamer for Capetown, Bombay, or Sydney; to transport her wardrobe and nursery to Downing Street; or to accompany her husband for the week-end to Windsor. On all these occasions she had obeyed her directions with efficiency and without surprise. Becomingly and suitably dressed, she had been ready at any moment to stand on quay or platform, waiting until fetched beside a pile of luggage. Herbert saw no reason now to doubt that his mother would dole out her time according to schedule in the spare bedrooms of her sons and daughters.

When he had finished, she said: 'That's very thoughtful of you, Herbert. It would be very kind of you to put this house in the agents' hands to-morrow.'

'Capital!' said Herbert; 'I'm so glad you agree. But you need not feel hurried. No doubt some little time must elapse before the house is sold. Mabel and I will expect you at your convenience.' And he stooped and patted her hand.

'Oh, but wait,' said Lady Slane, raising it. It was the first gesture she had made. 'You go too fast, Herbert. I don't agree.'

They all looked at her in consternation.

33

'You don't agree, Mother?'

'No,' said Lady Slane, smiling. 'I am not going to live with you, Herbert; nor with you, Carrie; nor with you, William; nor with you, Charles, kind though you all are. I am going to live by myself.'

'By yourself, Mother? It's impossible – and anyway, where would you live?'

'At Hampstead,' replied Lady Slane, nodding her head quietly, as though in response to an inner thought.

'At Hampstead? – but will you find a house that will suit you; convenient, and not too dear? – Really,' said Carrie, 'here we are discussing Mother's house as though everything were settled. It is absurd. I don't know what has come over us.'

'There is a house,' said Lady Slane, again nodding her head; 'I have seen it.'

'But, Mother, you haven't been to Hampstead.' This was intolerable. Carrie had known all her mother's movements day by day for the past fifteen years at least, and she revolted against the suggestion that her mother had visited Hampstead without her knowledge. Such a hint of independence was an outrage, almost a manifesto. There had always been so close and continuous a connection between Lady Slane and her eldest daughter; the plans for the day would always be arranged between them; Genoux would be sent round with a note in the morning; or they would telephone, at great length; or Carrie would come round to Elm Park Gardens after breakfast, tall, practical, rustling, self-important, equipped for the day with her gloves, her hat, and her boa, a shopping list slipped into her bag, and the agenda papers for the afternoon's committee, and the two elderly ladies would talk over the day's doings while Lady Slane went on with her knitting, and then they would go out together at about half-past eleven, two tall figures in black, familiar to the other old ladies of the neighbourhood; or if their business, for once, did not lie in the same direction, Carrie would at least drop into Elm Park Gardens for tea, and would learn exactly how her mother had spent her day. It was surely impossible that Lady Slane should have concealed an expedition to Hampstead.

'Thirty years ago,' said Lady Slane. 'I saw the house then.' She took a skein of wool from her work-basket and held it out to Kay. 'Hold it for me, please, Kay,' and after first carefully breaking the little loops she began to wind. She was the very incarnation of placidity. 'I am sure the house is still there,' she said, carefully winding, and Kay with the experience of long habit stood before her, moving his hands rhythmically up and down, so that the wool might slip off his fingers without catching. 'I am sure the house is still there,' she said, and her tone was a mixture between dreaminess and confidence, as though she had some secret understanding with the house, and it were waiting for her, patient, after thirty years; 'it was a convenient little house,' she added prosaically, 'not too small and not too large – Genoux could manage it single-handed I think, with perhaps a daily char to do the rough work – and there was a nice garden, with peaches against the wall, looking south. It was to be let when I saw it, but of course your father would not have liked that. I remember the name of the agent.'

'And what,' snapped Carrie, 'was the name of the agent?'

'It was a funny name,' said Lady Slane, 'perhaps that's why I remember it. Bucktrout. Gervase Bucktrout. It seemed to go so well with the house.'

'Oh,' said Mabel, clasping her hands, 'I think it sounds too delicious – peaches, and Bucktrout . . .'

'Be quiet, Mabel,' said Herbert. 'Of course, my dear Mother, if you are set on this – ah – eccentric scheme, there is no more to be said about it. You are entirely your own mistress, after all. But will it not look a little odd in the eyes of the world, when you have so many devoted children, that you should elect to live alone in retirement at Hampstead? Far be it from me to wish to press you, of course.'

'I don't think so, Herbert,' said Lady Slane, and having come to the end of her winding, she said, 'Thank you, Kay,' and making a loop on a long knitting needle she started on a fresh piece of knitting. 'Lots of old ladies live in retirement at Hampstead. Besides, I have considered the eyes of the world for so long that I think it is time I had a little holiday from them. If one is not to please oneself in old age, when is one to please oneself? There is so little time left!'

'Well,' said Carrie, making the best of a bad job, 'at least we shall see to it that you are never lonely. There are so many of us that we can easily arrange for you to have at least one visitor a day. Though, to be sure, Hampstead is a long way off, and it is not always easy to fit in the arrangements about the motor,' she added, looking meaningly at her small husband, who quailed. 'But there are always the great-grandchildren,' she said, brightening; 'you'd like to have them coming in and out, keeping you in touch; I know you wouldn't be happy without that.'

'On the contrary,' said Lady Slane, 'that is another thing about which I have made up my mind. You see, Carrie, I am going to become completely self-indulgent. I am going to wallow in old age. No grandchildren. They are too young. Not one of them has reached forty-five. No great-grandchildren either; that would be worse. I want no strenuous young people, who are not content with doing a thing, but must needs know why they do it. And I don't want them bringing their children to see me, for it would only remind me of the terrible effort the poor creatures will have to make before they reach the end of their lives in safety. I prefer to forget about them. I want no one about me except those who are nearer to their death than to their birth.'

36

Herbert, Carrie, Charles, and William decided that their mother must be mad. They took a step forward, and from having always thought her simple, decided that old age had definitely affected her brain. Her madness, however, was taking a harmless and even a convenient form. William might be thinking rather regretfully of the lost subsidy to his house-books, Carrie and Herbert might remain still a little dubious about the eyes of the world, but, on the whole, it was a relief to find their mother settling her own affairs. Kay gazed inquiringly at his mother. He had taken her so much for granted; they had all taken her so much for granted – her gentleness, her unselfishness, her impersonal activities – and now, for the first time in his life, it was becoming apparent to Kay that people could still hold surprises up their sleeves, however long one had known them. Edith alone frolicked in her mind. She thought her mother not mad, but most conspicuously sane. She was delighted to see Carrie and Herbert routed, by their mother quietly disentangling herself from their toils. Softly she clapped her hands together, and whispered 'Go on, Mother! go on!' Only a remnant of prudence prevented her from saying it out loud. She revelled in her mother's new-found eloquence – not the least of the surprises of that surprising morning, for Lady Slane habitually was reserved in speech, withholding her opinion, concealing even the expression on her face as she bent her head over her knitting or embroidery, when her occasional 'Yes, dear?' gave but little indication of what she was really thinking. It now dawned upon Edith that her mother might have lived a full private life, all these years, behind the shelter of her affectionate watchfulness. How much had she observed? noted? criticised? stored up? She was speaking again, rummaging meanwhile in her work-bag.

'I have taken the jewels out of the bank, Herbert. You and Mabel had better have them. I wanted to give them to Mabel years ago, but your father objected. However, here are some of them,' and as she spoke she turned the bag over and shook the contents out on to her lap, a careless assortment of leather cases, tissue paper, some loose stones, and skeins of wool. With her fine hands she began picking them over. 'Ring the bell for Genoux, Edith,' she said, glancing up. 'I never cared about jewels, you know,' she said, speaking to herself rather than to her family at large, 'and it seemed such a pity – such a waste – that so many should have come my way. Your father used to say that I must be able to deck myself out on Occasions. When we were in India, he used to buy back a lot of things at the Tash-i-Khane auctions. He had a theory that it pleased the princes to see me wearing their gifts, even though they knew perfectly well that we had bought them back. I daresay he was right. But it always seemed rather silly to me – such a farce. I had a big topaz once, a big bronze topaz, unset, cut into dozens of facets; I wonder if you children remember it? I used to make you look at the fire through it. It made hundreds of little flames; some went the right way up, and others upside down. When you came down after tea we used to sit in front of the fire looking through it, like Nero at the burning of Rome. Only it was brown fire, not green. I don't suppose you remember. That was sixty years ago. I lost it, of course; one always does lose the things one values most. I never lost any of the other things; perhaps because Genoux always had charge of them – and she used to invent the most extraordinary places to hide them in – she mistrusted safes, so she used to drop my diamonds into the cold water jug – no robber would think of looking for them there, she said. I often thought that if Genoux died suddenly I shouldn't know where to look for the jewels myself – but the topaz I used to carry in my pocket.' Here Lady Slane's dreamy reminiscences were cut short as Genoux came in, rustling like a snake in dry leaves, creaking like a saddle, for, until May was out, Genoux would not abandon the layers of brown paper that reinforced her corsets and her combinations against the English climate. 'Miladi a sonné?'

Yes, thought Edith, there's nobody here for Genoux but Mother; only Mother can have rung the bell; only Mother can have an order to give, though we are all assembled: Herbert peeking over his collar, Carrie drawing herself up, outraged, Charles twisting his moustaches like somebody sharpening a pencil – though who cares for Charles? not even the War Office, and Charles knows it. They all know that nobody cares for them; that's why they talk so loud. Mother has never talked at all – until to-day; yet Genoux comes in as though Mother were the only person in the room, in the house, fit to give an order. Genoux knows where respect is due. Genoux takes no account of insistent voices. 'Miladi a sonné?'

'Genoux, vous avez les bijoux?'

'Mais bien sûr, miladi, que j'ai les bijoux. J'appelle ça le trésor. Miladi veut que j'aille chercher le trésor?'

'Please, Genoux,' said Lady Slane, determined, though Genoux sent a glance round the family circle as though Herbert, Carrie, Charles, William, Lavinia, and even the snubbed and innocuous Mabel were the very robbers against whose coming she had dropped the diamonds nightly into the jug of cold water. Indian verandahs and South African stoeps had, in the past, whispered in Genoux's imagination with the stealthy footsteps of robbers bent upon the viceregal jewels – 'ces sales nègres;' – but now a more immediate, because a more legitimate and English, danger menaced these jealously guarded possessions. Miladi, so gentle, so vague, so detached, could never be trusted to look after herself or her belongings. Genoux was by nature a watchdog. 'Miladi se souviendra au moins que les bagues lui ont été très spécialement données par ce pauvre milord?'

Lady Slane looked down at her hands. They were, as the

39

saying goes, loaded with rings. That saying means, in so far as any saying means anything at all – and every saying, every *cliché*, once meant something tightly related to some human experience – that the gems concerned were too weighty for the hands that bore them. Her hands were indeed loaded with rings. They had been thus loaded by Lord Slane – tokens of affection, certainly, but no less tokens of the embellishments proper to the hands of Lord Slane's wife. The great half-hoop of diamonds twisted round easily upon her finger. (Lord Slane had been wont to observe that his wife's hands were as soft as doves; which was true in a way, since they melted into nothing as one clasped them; and in another way was quite untrue, since to the outward eye they were fine, sculptural, and characteristic; but Lord Slane might be trusted to seize upon the more feminine aspect, and to ignore the subtler, less convenient, suggestion.) Lady Slane, then, looked down at her hands as though Genoux had for the first time drawn attention to them. For one's hands are the parts of one's body that one suddenly sees with the maximum of detachment; they are suddenly far off; and one observes their marvellous articulations, and miraculous response to the transmission of instantaneous messages, as though they belonged to another person, or to another piece of machinery; one observes even the oval of their nails, the pores of their skin, the wrinkles of their phalanges and knuckles, their smoothness or rugosities, with an estimating and interested eye; they have been one's servants, and yet one has not investigated their personality; a personality which, cheiromancy assures us, is so much bound up with our own. One sees them also, as the case may be, loaded with rings or rough with work. So did Lady Slane look down upon her hands. They had been with her all her life, those hands. They had grown with her from the chubby hands of a child to the ivory-smooth hands of an old woman. She twisted the half-hoop of diamonds, and the half-hoop of rubies, loosely and reminiscently. She had worn them for so long that they had become a part of her. 'No, Genoux,' she said, 'soyez sans crainte; I know the rings are mine.'

But the other things were not hers in the same way; and indeed she did not want them. Genoux produced them one after the other, and handed them over to Herbert, counting, as a peasant might count out a clutch of eggs to the buyer. Herbert, for his part, received them and passed them on to Mabel much as a bricklayer passing on bricks to his mate. He had a sense of value, but none of beauty. Lady Slane sat by, watching. She had a sense of beauty, though none of value. The cost of these things, their marketable price, meant nothing to her. Their beauty meant much, though she felt no proprietary interest; and their associations meant much, representing as they did the whole background of her life in its most fantastic aspect. Those sceptres of jade, brought by the emissaries of the Tibetan Lama! how well she remembered the ceremony of their presentation, when the yellow-coated emissaries, squatting, had drawn howls of music from bones the length of a mammoth's thigh. And she remembered checking her amusement, even while she sat conformably beside the Viceroy in his Durbar Hall, checking it with the thought that it was on a par with the narrow English amusement at the unfamiliar collection of consonants in a Polish name. What, save their unfamiliarity, caused her to smile at the wails drawn from a Tibetan thighbone? Kubelik might equally cause a Tibetan lama to smile. Then the Indian princes had come with their gifts that now Genoux delivered over to Herbert, the heir, in Elm Park Gardens. The Indian princes had known very well that their gifts would be pooled in the Tash-i-Khane, to be bought back according to the Viceroy's purse and discretion. Knobbly pearls, and uncut emeralds, heavily flawed, passed now between

Genoux's resentful hands and Herbert's, decently avid. Red velvet cases opened to display bracelets and necklaces; 'tout est bien en ordre,' said Genoux, snapping the cases shut. A small table was quite covered with cases by the time they had finished. 'My dear Mabel,' said Lady Slane, 'I had better lend you a portmanteau.'

Loot. The eyes of William and Lavinia glittered. Lady Slane remained oblivious of their covetous glances, and of their resentment at this one-sided distribution. Not so much as a brooch for Lavinia! It had simply never occurred to Lady Slane that she ought to divide the things; that was obvious. Lavinia and Carrie watched in silent rage. Such simplicity amounted to imbecility. But Herbert was well aware, and – so amiable are our secret feelings – rejoiced. He enjoyed their discomfiture, and further to increase it addressed Mabel quite affectionately for once: 'Put on the pearls, my dear; I am sure they will be most becoming.' Becoming they were not, to Mabel's faded little face, for Mabel who had once been pretty had now faded, according to the penalty of fair people, so that her skin appeared to be darker than her hair, and her hair without lustre, the colour of dust. The pearls, which had once dripped their sheen among the laces and softnesses of Lady Slane, now hung in a dispirited way round Mabel's scraggy neck. 'Very nice, dear Mabel,' said Lavinia, putting up her lorgnon; 'but how odd it is, isn't it, that these Oriental presents should always be of such poor quality? Those pearls are quite yellow, really, now that I come to look at them – more like old piano keys. I never noticed that before, when your mother wore them.'

'About the house, Mother,' began Carrie. 'Would to-morrow suit you to see it? I think I have a free afternoon,' and she began to consult a small diary taken from her bag.

'Thank you, Carrie,' said Lady Slane, setting the crown upon the surprises she had already given them, 'but I have made an appointment to see the house to-morrow. And, although it is very nice of you to offer, I think I will go there alone.'

It was something of an adventure for Lady Slane to go alone to Hampstead, and she felt happier after safely changing trains at Charing Cross. An existence once limited only by the boundaries of Empire had shrunk since the era of Elm Park Gardens began. Or perhaps she was one of those people on whom a continuous acquaintance with strange countries makes little impression – they remain themselves to the end; or perhaps she was really getting old. At the age of eighty-eight one might be permitted to say it. This consciousness, this sensation, of age was curious and interesting. The mind was as alert as ever, perhaps more alert, sharpened by the sense of imminent final interruption, spurred by the necessity of making the most of remaining time; only the body was a little shaky, not very certain of its reliability, not quite certain even of its sense of direction, afraid of stumbling over a step, of spilling a cup of tea; nervous, tremulous; aware that it must not be jostled, or hurried, for fear of betraying its frail inadequacy. Younger people did not always seem to notice or to make allowance; and when they did notice they were apt to display a slight irritability, dawdling rather too markedly in order to keep pace with the hesitant footsteps. For that reason Lady Slane had never much enjoyed her walks with Carrie to the corner where they caught the bus. Yet, going up to Hampstead alone, she did not feel old; she felt younger than she had felt for years, and the proof of it was that she accepted eagerly this start of a new lap in life, even though it be the last. Nor did she look her age, as she sat, swaying slightly with the rocking of the Underground train, very upright, clasping her umbrella and her bag, her ticket carefully pushed into the opening of her glove. It did not occur to her to wonder what her travelling companions would think, could they know that two days previously she had buried her husband in Westminster Abbey. She was more immediately concerned with the extraordinary sensation of being independent of Carrie.

(Leicester Square.)

How Henry's death had brought about this sudden emancipation she could not conceive. It was just another instance of what she had vaguely noted all her life: how certain events brought apparently irrelevant results in their train. She had once asked Henry whether the same phenomenon were observable in the realm of politics, but although he had accorded her (as always, and to everyone) the gravest courtesy of his attention, he had obviously failed to understand what she meant. Yet Henry rarely failed to pick up the meaning of what people said. On the contrary, he would let them talk, keeping his keen humorous eyes upon them all the while, and then he would pick out the central point of their meaning, however clumsily they had indicated it, and, catching it up between his hands, would toss it about as a juggler with golden balls, until from a poor poverty-stricken thing it became a spray, a fountain, full of glitter and significance under the play of his incomparable intelligence – for this was the remarkable, the attractive thing about Henry, the thing which made people call him the most charming man in the world: that he gave the best of his intelligence to everybody on the slightest demand, whether a Cabinet Minister at the council table, or an intimidated young woman sitting next to him at dinner. He was never dismissive, perfunctory, or contemptuous. He seized upon any subject, however trivial; and the further removed from his own work or interests the better. He would discuss ball-dresses with a débutante, polo ponies with a subaltern, or Beethoven with either. Thus he deluded legions of people into believing that they had really secured his interest.

44

(Tottenham Court Road.)

But, when his wife asked him that question about events and irrelevant results, he was not disposed to take the matter up, and had played instead with the rings on her fingers. She could see the rings now, making bumps under her black gloves. She sighed. Often she had pressed a tentative switch, and Henry's mind had failed to light up. She had accepted this at last, taking refuge in the thought that she was probably the only person in the world with whom he need not make an effort. It was perhaps an arid compliment, but a sincere one. She regretted it now: there were so many things she would have liked to discuss with Henry; impersonal things, nothing troublesome. She had had that unique opportunity, that potential privilege, for nearly seventy years, and now it was gone, flattened under the slabs of Westminster Abbey.

(Goodge Street.)

He would have been amused by her emancipation from Carrie. He had never liked Carrie; she doubted whether he had ever much liked any of his children. He never criticised anybody – that was one of his characteristics – but Lady Slane knew him well enough (although in a sense she did not know him at all) to know when he approved of a person and when he did not. His commendations were always measured; but, conversely, when withheld, their absence meant a great deal. She could not recollect one word of approval for Carrie, unless 'Damned efficient woman, my daughter,' could be counted as approval. The expression in his eye whenever he looked at Herbert had been unmistakable; nor had Charles ever succeeded in obtaining much sympathy from his father in his many grievances. (Euston.) Lord Slane had been apt to consider his son, the General, with an air of as-much-as-to-say, 'Now shall I bestir myself and give this rhetorical and peevish man my exact opinion of government offices, about which, after all, I know a great deal more than he does, or shall I not?' So far as Lady Slane knew he never had. He had preferred to endure in silence. William he quite markedly avoided, though Lady Slane, with dishonest loyalty for her own son, had always tried to attribute this avoidance to a dislike of Lavinia. 'My dear,' Henry had once said, under pressure of exhortation, 'I find it difficult to accommodate myself to the society of minds balanced like a ledger,' and Lady Slane had sighed, and had said yes, it must be admitted that Lavinia had done poor William's nature a certain amount of harm. At which Lord Slane had replied, 'Harm? they are two peas in a pod,' which, for him, was a tart rejoinder.

(Camden Town.)

For Edith he had had a somewhat selfish affection. She had remained at home; she had been obliging; she had taken him for walks; she had answered some of his letters. True, she had often muddled them; had sent them off unsigned, or, if signed, without an address, in which case they had been returned through the Dead Letter Office to 'Slane, Elm Park Gardens,' a contretemps which always caused Lord Slane more amusement than annoyance. Never had Lord Slane had occasion to call his daughter Edith a damned efficient woman. Lady Slane had sometimes been tempted to think that he liked Edith more for the opportunities she afforded him of teasing her than for the reliance he placed upon her well-intentioned service.

(Chalk Farm.)

Kay. But before Lady Slane could consider what Lord Slane had made of that curious problem Kay, before she could pull up yet another fish of memory on a long line, she recollected a restriction she had placed upon herself, namely, not to let her memory wander until the days of complete leisure should be come; not to luxuriate until she could luxuriate fully and freely. Her feast must not be spoiled by snippets of anticipation. The

46

train itself came to her assistance, for, after jerking over points, it ran into yet another white-tiled station, where a line of red tiles framed the name: Hampstead. Lady Slane rose unsteadily to her feet, reaching out her hand for a helpful bar; it was on these occasions and these alone, when she must compete with the rush of mechanical life, that she betrayed herself for an old lady. She became then a little tremulous, a little afraid. It became apparent that in her frailty she dreaded being bustled. Yet, in her anxiety not to inconvenience others, she always took conductors at their word and hurried obediently when they shouted, 'Hurry along, please'; as, again, in her anxiety not to push herself forward, she always allowed others to board the train or the bus while she herself hung courteously back. Many a train and bus she had missed by this method, often to the exasperation of Carrie, who had invariably secured her own place, and was borne away, seeing her mother left standing on platform or pavement.

It was a wonder, arrived at Hampstead, that Lady Slane descended from the train in time, successfully clasping her umbrella, her bag, and her ticket inside her glove, but descend she did, and found herself standing in the warm summer air with the roofs of London beneath her. The passers-by ignored her, standing there, so well accustomed were they to the sight of old ladies in Hampstead. Setting out to walk, she wondered if she remembered the way; but Hampstead seemed scarcely a part of London, so sleepy and village-like, with its warm red-brick houses and vistas of trees and distance that reminded her pleasantly of Constable's paintings. She walked slowly but happily, and without anxiety, as in a friendly retreat, no longer thinking of Henry's opinion of his children, or indeed of anything but the necessity of finding the house, *her* house, which thirty years ago had been one of just such a red-brick row, with its garden behind it. It was curious to think that she would see it again, so imminently. Thirty years. Ten years longer than the span needed for a baby to grow up into full consciousness. Who could tell what might have happened to the house during that span? whether it had seen turmoil, desolation, or merely placidity?

The house had indeed been waiting several years for someone to come and inhabit it. It had been let once only since Lady Slane first saw it, thirty years ago, to a quiet old couple with no more history than the ordinary history of human beings – eventful enough, God knows, in their own eyes, but so usual as to merge unrecorded into the general sea of lives – a quiet old couple, their peripeteias left behind them; they had come there to fade slowly, to drift gently out of existence, and so they had faded, so they had drifted; they had, in fact, both drawn their last breath in the bedroom facing south, above the peaches – so the caretaker told Lady Slane, by way of encouragement, snapping up the blinds and letting in the sun, in an off-hand way, talking meanwhile, and wiping a cobweb off the window-sill with a sweep of her lifted apron, and looking back at Lady Slane as much as to say, 'There, now, you can see what it's like – not much to look at – just a house to let – make up your mind quickly, for goodness' sake, and let me get back to my tea.' But Lady Slane, standing in the deserted room, said quietly that she had an appointment with Mr Bucktrout.

The caretaker might go, she said; there was no need for her to wait; and some note of viceregal authority must have lingered in her voice, for the caretaker's antagonism changed to a sort of bedraggled obsequiousness. All the same, she said, she must lock up. There were the keys. Day in, day out, she had unlocked the house, flicked it over with a hasty duster, and locked it up again, to return to its silence and the occasional fall of plaster from the walls. During the night the plaster had fallen, and must be swept up in the morning. It was terrible the state an unoccupied house got into. The very ivy came creeping in between the windows; Lady Slane looked at it, a pale young frond waving listlessly in the sunshine. Bits of straw blew about on the floor. An enormous spider scuttled quickly, ran up the wall, and vanished into a crevice. Yes, said Lady Slane, the caretaker might go, and no doubt Mr Bucktrout would be so kind as to lock up.

The caretaker shrugged. After all, there was nothing in the house for Lady Slane to steal, and she wanted her tea. Receiving a tip of half-a-crown, she went. Lady Slane was left alone in the house; she heard the front door slam as the caretaker went away. How wrongly caretakers were named: they took so little care. A perfunctory banging about with black water in a galvanised pail, a dirty clout smeared over the floor, and they thought their work was done. Small blame to them, perhaps, receiving a few shillings a week and expected to make their knuckles even more unsightly in the care of a house which, to them, was at best a job and at worst a nuisance. One could not demand of them that they should give the care which comes from the heart. Very few months of such toil would blunt one's zeal, and caretakers had a lifetime of it. Nor could one expect them to feel how strange a thing a house was, especially an empty house; not merely a systematic piling-up of brick on brick, regulated in the building by plumb-line and spirit-level, pierced at intervals by doors and casements, but an entity with a life of its own, as though some unifying breath were blown into the air confined within this square brick box, there to remain until the prisoning walls should fall away, exposing it to a general publicity. It was a very private thing, a house; private with a privacy irrespective of bolts and bars. And if this superstition seemed irrational, one might reply that man himself was but a collection of atoms, even as a house was but a collection of bricks, yet man laid claim to a soul, to a spirit, to a power of recording and of perception, which had no more to do with his restless atoms than had the house with its stationary bricks. Such beliefs were beyond rational explanation; one could not expect a caretaker to take them into account.

Lady Slane experienced the curious sensation common to all who remain alone for the first time in an empty house which may become their home. She gazed out of the first-floor window, but her mind ran up and down the stairs and peeped into rooms, for already, at this her first visit, the geography had impressed itself familiarly; that in itself was a sign that she and the house were in accord. It ran down even into the cellar, where she had not descended, but whose mossy steps she had seen; and she wondered idly whether fungi grew there – not the speckled orange sort but the bleached kind – unwholesome in a more unpleasant way. It seemed likely that fungi should be included among the invaders of the house, and this brought her back to the bare room in which she stood, with its impudent inhabitants blowing, waving, running, as they listed.

These things – the straw, the ivy frond, the spider – had had the house all to themselves for many days. They had paid no rent, yet they had made free with the floor, the window, and the walls, during a light and volatile existence. That was the kind of companionship that Lady Slane wanted; she had had enough of bustle, and of competition, and of one set of ambitions writhing to circumvent another. She wanted to merge with the things that drifted into an empty house, though unlike the spider she would weave no webs. She would be content to stir with the breeze and grow green in the light of the sun, and to drift down the passage of years, until death pushed her gently out and shut the door behind her. She wanted nothing but passivity while these outward things worked their will upon her. But, first of all, it was necessary to know whether she could have the house.

A slight sound downstairs – was it the opening of a door? – made her listen. Mr Bucktrout? Her appointment with him was for half-past four, and the hour was already struck. She must see him, she supposed, though she hated business, and would have preferred to take possession of the house as the straw, the ivy, and the spider had taken possession, simply adding herself to their number. She sighed, foreseeing a lot of business before she could sit at peace in the garden; documents would have to be signed, orders given, curtains and carpets chosen, and various human beings set in motion, all provided with hammers, tintacks, needles, and thread, before she and her belongings could settle down after their last journey. Why could one not possess the ring of Aladdin? Simplify life as one might, one could not wholly escape its enormous complication.

The thought struck her that the Mr Bucktrout whose name she had noted thirty years ago might well have been replaced by some efficient young son, and great was her relief when, peeping over the banisters, she saw, curiously foreshortened to her view, a safely old gentleman standing in the hall. She looked down on his bald patch; below that she saw his shoulders, no body to speak of, and then two patent-leather toes. He stood there hesitant; perhaps he did not know that his client had already arrived, perhaps he did not care. She thought it more probable that he did not care. He appeared to be in no hurry to find out. Lady Slane crept down a few steps, that she might get a better view of him. He wore a long linen coat like a housepainter's; he had a rosy and somewhat chubby face, and he held one finger pressed against his lips, as though archly and impishly preoccupied with some problem in his mind. What on earth is he going to do, she wondered, observing this strange little figure. Still pressing his finger, as though enjoining silence, he tiptoed across the hall to where a stain on the wall indicated that a barometer had once hung there; then rapidly tapped the wall like a woodpecker tapping a tree; shook his head; muttered 'Falling! falling!'; and, picking up the skirts of his coat, he executed two neat pirouettes which brought him back to the centre of the hall, his foot pointed nicely before him.

'Mr Bucktrout?' said Lady Slane, descending.

Mr Bucktrout gave a skip and changed the foot pointed before him. He paused to admire his instep. Then he looked up. 'Lady Slane?' he said, performing a bow full of elaborate courtesy.

'I came about the house,' said Lady Slane, quite at her ease and drawn by an instant sympathy to this eccentric person.

Mr Bucktrout dropped his skirts and stood on two feet like anybody else. 'Ah yes, the house,' he said; 'I had forgotten. One must be business-like, although the glass is falling. So you want to see the house, Lady Slane. It is a nice house – so nice that I wouldn't care to let it to everybody. It is my own house, you understand; I am the owner, as well as the agent. If I had been merely the agent, acting on the owner's behalf, I should have felt it my duty to let when I could. That is why it has remained empty for so long. I have had many applicants, but I liked none of them. But you shall see it.' He put a slight emphasis on the 'you'.

'I have seen it,' said Lady Slane; 'the caretaker showed me over.'

'Of course. A horrid woman. So harsh, so sordid. Did you give her a tip?'

'Yes,' said Lady Slane, amused. 'I gave her half-a-crown.'

'Ah, that's a pity. Too late now, though. Well, you have seen the house. Have you seen it all? Bedrooms, three; bathroom, one; lavatories, two, one upstairs and one down; reception rooms, three; lounge hall; usual offices. Company's water; electric light. Half an acre of garden; ancient fruit-trees, including a mulberry. Fine cellar; do you care for mushrooms? you could grow mushrooms in the cellar. Ladies, I find, seldom care much for wine, so the cellar might as well be used for mushrooms. I have never yet met with a lady who troubled to lay down a pipe of port. And so, Lady Slane, having seen the house, what do you think of it?'

Lady Slane hesitated, as the fanciful idea crossed her mind of telling Mr Bucktrout the exact thoughts which had occurred to her while she awaited him; she felt confident that he would receive them with complete gravity and without surprise. But, instead, she confined herself to saying with the approved caution and reticence of a potential tenant, 'I think it would probably suit me very well.'

'Ah, but the question is,' said Mr Bucktrout, again putting his finger to his lips, 'will you suit *it*? I have a feeling that you might. And, in any case, you would not want it after the end of the world.'

'I expect my own end will come before that,' said Lady Slane, smiling.

'Not unless you are very old indeed,' said Mr Bucktrout seriously. 'The end of the world is due in two years' time – I could convince you by a few simple mathematical calculations. Perhaps you are no mathematician. Few ladies are. But if the subject interests you I could come to tea with you one day when you are established and give you my demonstration.'

'So I am going to be established here, am I?' said Lady Slane.

'I think so – yes – I think so,' said Mr Bucktrout, putting his head on one side and looking obliquely at her. 'It seems likely. Otherwise, why should you have remembered the house for thirty years – you said so in your letter – and why should I have turned away so many tenants? The two things seem to come together, do they not, to converge at a point, after describing separate arcs? I am a great believer in the geometrical designs of destiny. That is another thing I should like to demonstrate to you one day if I may come to tea. Of course, if I were only the agent I should never suggest coming to tea. It would not be meet. But, being also the owner, I feel that once we have finished all our business we may meet upon an equal footing.'

'Indeed, I hope you will come whenever you feel inclined, Mr Bucktrout,' said Lady Slane.

'You are most gracious, Lady Slane. I have few friends, and I find that as one grows older one relies more and more on the society of one's contemporaries and shrinks from the society of the young. They are so tiring. So unsettling. I can scarcely, nowadays, endure the company of anybody under seventy. Young people compel one to look forward on a life full of effort. Old people permit one to look backward on a life whose effort is over and done with. That is reposeful. Repose, Lady Slane, is one of the most important things in life, yet how few people achieve it? How few people, indeed, desire it? The old have it imposed upon them. Either they are infirm, or weary. But half of them still sigh for the energy which once was theirs. Such a mistake.'

'That, at any rate, is a mistake of which I am not guilty,' said Lady Slane, betraying herself with relief to Mr Bucktrout.

'No? Then we are agreed upon at least one of the major subjects. It is terrible to be twenty, Lady Slane. It is as bad as being faced with riding over the Grand National course. One knows one will almost certainly fall into the Brook of Competition, and break one's leg over the Hedge of Disappointment, and stumble over the Wire of Intrigue, and quite certainly come to grief over the Obstacle of Love. When one is old, one can throw oneself down as a rider on the evening after the race, and think, Well, I shall never have to ride that course again.'

'But you forget, Mr Bucktrout,' said Lady Slane, delving into

54

her own memories, 'when one was young, one enjoyed living dangerously – one desired it – one wasn't appalled.'

'Yes,' said Mr Bucktrout, 'that is true. When I was a young man I was a Hussar. My greatest pleasure was pig-sticking. I assure you, Lady Slane, that I touched the highest moment of life whenever I saw a fine pair of tusks coming at me. I have several pairs, mounted, in my house to-day, which I should be pleased to show you. But I had no ambition – no military ambition. I never had the slightest wish to command my regiment. So of course I resigned my commission, since when I have learnt that the pleasures of contemplation are greater than the pleasures of activity.'

The image of Mr Bucktrout as a Hussar, thus evoked by his queerly stilted phrases, moved Lady Slane to an amusement which she was careful to conceal. She found it easy to believe that he had never cherished any military ambition. She found him entirely to her liking. Still, it was necessary to recall him to practical matters, she supposed, though heaven knows that this rambling conversation was for her a new and luxurious indulgence. 'But now, about the house, Mr Bucktrout,' she began, much as Carrie had resumed the topic with herself after that flow of passing jewels; it was a relapse into the old viceregal manner that brought Mr Bucktrout back from pig-sticking in the scrub to the subject of rents in Hampstead. 'I like the house,' said Lady Slane, 'and apparently,' she added with a smile that undid the viceregal manner, 'you approve of me as a tenant. But what about business? What about the rent?'

He gave her a startled look; evidently, he had been busy pig-sticking by himself in the interval; had returned to life as a Hussar, forgetting himself as owner and agent. He put his finger to his nose this time, quizzing Lady Slane, giving himself time to think. The subject seemed distasteful to him, though relics of a business training tugged at him, jerking some string in his mind; he lived, naturally, in a world where rents were not of much importance. So did Lady Slane; and thus a pair more ill-assorted, and yet better assorted, to discuss rents could scarcely be imagined. 'The rent ... the rent ...' said Mr Bucktrout, as one who endeavours to establish connection with some word in a foreign language he once has known.

Then he brightened. 'Of course: the rent,' he said briskly. 'You want to take the house on a yearly tenancy?' he said, recovering his vocabulary after his excursion of fifty years back into his pig-sticking days as a Hussar. 'It would scarcely be worth your while,' he added, 'to take it on more than a yearly tenancy. You might vacate it at any moment, and your heirs would not wish to have it on their hands. I think that on that basis we might come to a satisfactory agreement. I like the idea of a tenant who will give me recovery of the house within a short period. Apart from my personal predilection for you, Lady Slane, abruptly sprung though that predilection may be, I relish the idea that this particular house should return at short intervals again into my keeping. From that point of view alone, you would suit me admirably as a tenant. There are other points of view, of course – as in this life there invariably are – but in the interests of business I must for the present ignore them. Those other points of view are purely sentimental – *ee gee*, that I should fancy you as the occupier of this particular house (speaking as the owner, not the agent), and that I may look forward to agreeable afternoons at tea-time when I may set before you, as a lady of understanding, my several little demonstrations. Those considerations must stand aside for the moment. We are here to discuss the question of rent.' He pointed a foot; recollected himself; took it back; and cocked at Lady Slane an eye full of satisfaction and triumph.

He puts it delicately, admirably, thought Lady Slane; it would scarcely be worth my while to take the house on more than a yearly tenancy, since at any moment I might vacate it by being carried out of it in my coffin. But what if he should pre-decease me? for although I am certainly an old woman, he is equally certainly an old man. Any delicacy of speech between people so near to death, is surely absurd? But people do not willingly speak in plain English of death, however fixedly its imminence may weigh on their hearts; so Lady Slane refrained from pointing out the possible fallacies of Mr Bucktrout's argument, and merely said, 'A yearly tenancy would suit me very well. Still, that doesn't reply to my inquiry about the rent?'

Mr Bucktrout was manifestly embarrassed at being thus chased into a corner. Although both owner and agent, he was one of those who resent seeing their fantasies reduced to terms of pounds and pence. Moreover, he had set his heart upon Lady Slane as a tenant. He temporised. 'Well, Lady Slane, I counter your inquiry. What rent would you be willing to pay?'

Delicacy again, thought Lady Slane. He doesn't say: 'What rent could you afford to pay?' This fencing, this walking round one another like two courting pigeons, was becoming ludicrous. Henry would have struck down between them, cleaving the situation with an axe of cold sense. Yet she liked the odd little man, and was thankful, heartily thankful, that she had rejected Carrie's company. Carrie, like her father, would drastically have intervened, shattering thereby a relationship which had grown up, creating itself, as swiftly and exquisitely as a little rigged ship of blown glass, each strand hardening instantly as it left the tube and met the air, yet remaining so brittle that a false note, jarring on the ethereal ripples, could splinter it. Shrinking, Lady Slane named a sum, too large; which Mr Bucktrout immediately halved, too small.

But between them they came to a settlement. Though it might not be everybody's method of conducting business, it suited them very well, and they parted very much pleased with each other.

Carrie found her mother curiously reticent about the house. Yes, she had seen it; yes, she had seen the agent; yes, she had arranged to take it. On a yearly tenancy. Carrie exclaimed. What if the agent got a better offer and turned her out? Lady Slane smiled wisely. The agent, she said, wouldn't turn her out. But, said Carrie, agents were such dreadfully grasping people – quite naturally – they had to be grasping – what guarantee had her mother that at the end of a year she might not be obliged to look for another house? Lady Slane said that she anticipated no such thing; Mr Bucktrout was not that kind of person. Well, but, said Carrie, exasperated, Mr Bucktrout had his living to make, hadn't he? Business wasn't based on philanthropy. And had her mother made any arrangements about repairs and decoration, she asked? whisking off on to another subject, since she gave up all hope of doing something about the lease; what about papering, and distempering, and leaks in the roof? Had her mother thought of that? Carrie, who had controlled all her mother's decisions for years, really suffered a frenzy of mortification and anxiety, intensified by her inability to give free rein to her indignation, for she could not reasonably assume authority over an old lady of eighty-eight, if that old lady chose suddenly to imply that having reached the age of eighty-eight she was capable of managing her affairs for herself. Carrie was sure that she was capable of nothing of the sort; apart from her consternation at seeing herself deposed, she was genuinely concerned at seeing her mother heading straight and unrescuable into the most terrible muddle. Lady Slane meanwhile replied calmly that Mr Bucktrout had promised to arrange with carpenters, painters, plumbers, and upholsterers on her behalf. It was kind of Carrie to worry, but quite unnecessary. She and Mr Bucktrout would manage everything between them.

Carrie felt that it was useless even to mention the word Estimate. Her mother seemed to have gone right away from her, into a world ruled not by sense but by sentiment. A world in which one took other people's delicacy and nice feelings for granted. A world which, as Carrie knew very well, bore no relation to anything on this planet. It was all a part of the same thing as her mother's extraordinary indifference and obtuseness about the jewels. Who, in their senses, would have handed over five, perhaps seven, thousand pounds' worth of jewels like that? Who, with any proper perception, would have failed to realise that Carrie and Lavinia ought to have at least a share? Not to mention Edith. They would not have grudged poor Edith a brooch. After all, Edith was Father's daughter. But her mother had given everything away, as though it were so much useless lumber, just as she had now delivered herself and her purse gaily into the hands of an old shark called Bucktrout.

Carrie, however, found great consolation in talking the matter over at immense and repetitive length with her relations. Their solidarity was thereby increased. They all thoroughly enjoyed their gatherings over the tea-table – tea was their favourite, perhaps because the cheapest, meal – and nobody minded how often somebody else said the same thing, even framed in the same words. They listened each time with renewed approval, nodding their heads as though some new and illuminating discovery had just been made. Carrie and her relations found great reassurance in assertion and re-assertion. Say a thing often enough, and it becomes true; by hammering in sufficient stakes of similar pattern they erected a stockade between themselves and the wild dangers of life. The phrase 'Mother is wonderful,' so prevalent between the death and the funeral, was rapidly replaced by the phrase 'Dear Mother – so hopeless over anything practical.' But having said that – and having said it with commendable perseverance, in Queen's Gate where William and Lavinia lived, in Lower Sloane Street where Carrie and Roland lived, in the Cromwell Road where Charles had his flat, in Cadogan Square where Herbert and Mabel lived – having said that, they were brought up short against their inability to cope with that softly hopeless Mother. So amenable, so malleable always, she had routed them completely – she, and her house at Hampstead, and her Mr Bucktrout. They had none of them seen Mr Bucktrout; they had none of them been allowed to see him; even Carrie had been rejected, and her offer of lifts in the motor; but his invisibility added only fuel to the fire of their mistrust. He became 'This man who has Got Hold of Mother.' If Lady Slane had not already given all the pearls, the jade, the rubies, and the emeralds in that haphazard fashion to Herbert and Mabel, they would have suspected her of handing them all over to Mr Bucktrout at Mr Bucktrout's suggestion. This Mr Bucktrout, with his vagueness about the lease, with his helpfulness about carpenters, painters, plumbers, and upholsterers – what could he be but a shark? At the very best, his motive resolved itself for Carrie and her family into the ominous word Commission.

Meanwhile, Mr Bucktrout had secured the services of Mr Gosheron.

'You must understand,' he said to this estimable tradesman, 'that Lady Slane, despite her high position, is a lady of limited means. It is not always safe, Mr Gosheron, to assume affluence in the aristocracy. Because a gentleman has been Viceroy of India and Prime Minister of England it does not mean that his relict is left well-off. Our public services, Mr Gosheron, are conducted on very different principles. Therefore it becomes incumbent on you, Mr Gosheron, to keep your estimate as low as is compatible with your own reasonable profit. As an agent, and also as an owner of property, I have some experience in such matters. And I assure you that I shall make it my business to check your estimates on Lady Slane's behalf as it were upon my own.'

Mr Gosheron assured Mr Bucktrout in return that he would never dream of taking advantage of her ladyship.

Genoux, from the first time that she saw him, took a fancy to Mr Gosheron. 'Voilà un monsieur,' she said, 'qui connaît son travail. Il sait par exemple,' she added, 'quels weights il faut mettre dans les rideaux. Et il sait faire de la peinture pour que ça ne stick pas. J'aime,' she added, 'le bon travail – pas trop cher, mais pas de pacotille.' Genoux and Lady Slane, liberated from Carrie, spent very happy days with Mr Bucktrout and Mr Gosheron. Lady Slane liked everything about Mr Gosheron, even to his appearance. He looked most respectable, and invariably wore an old bowler hat, green with age, which he never removed even in the house, but which, in order to show some respect to Lady Slane, he would tilt forward by the back brim, and would then resettle into place. His hair, which had once been brown, but now was grey and stringy, invariably became disarranged by this tilting of the hat, so that after the tilting a strand stuck out at the back, fascinating Lady Slane, but unnoticed by its owner. He carried a pencil always behind his ear, a pencil so broad and of so soft a lead that it could serve for nothing except making a mark across a plank of wood, but which Lady Slane never saw used for any other purpose than scratching his head. In him she quickly recognised one of those craftsmen who find fault with all work not carried out under their own auspices. 'That's a poor sort of contraption,' Mr Gosheron would mutter, examining the damper of the kitchen range. He contrived to imply always that, had the job been left to him, he would have managed it a great deal better. Nevertheless, he implied at the same time, a man of his experience could put it right; could improve, though not quite satisfactorily, on a thoroughly bad job. Silent as a rule, and subdued in the presence of Mr Bucktrout, he occasionally indulged in an outburst of his own. Lady Slane was especially delighted when he indulged in outbursts, such as his outbursts against asbestos-roofed sectional bungalows. These outbursts were the more valuable for their rarity. 'I can't understand, my lady,' he said, 'how people can live without beauty.' Mr Gosheron could see beauty in a deal board, if it were well-fitted, though naturally he preferred an oak one. 'And to think,' he said, 'that some people cover up the grain with paint!' Mr Gosheron was not a young man; he was seventy if a day, but his traditions went back a hundred years or more. 'These lorries,' he said, 'shaking down the walls!' Henry Slane, always progressive, had seen beauty in lorries even as Mr Gosheron saw it in a well-carpentered board; but Lady Slane, who for years had striven loyally to keep up with the beauty of lorries, now found herself released back into a far more congenial set of values. She could dally for hours with Mr Bucktrout and Mr Gosheron, with Genoux following them about as a solid and stocky chorus. Planted squarely on her two feet, creaking within her brown paper linings, Genoux who had spent her life disapproving on principle of nearly everybody, regarded Mr Bucktrout and Mr Gosheron with an approval amounting almost to love. How different they were, how puzzlingly, pleasingly different, from the children of miladi! – for whom, nevertheless, Genoux nourished an awed respect. The two old gentlemen seemed so genuinely anxious that Lady Slane should have everything just as she liked it, yet should be spared all possible expense; when she made tentative suggestions, as to the inclusion of a glass shelf in the bathroom, or whatever it might be, they looked at each other with a glance of confederacy, almost a wink, and invariably said they thought that could be managed. That was the way Genoux liked to see miladi treated – as though she were something precious, and fragile, and unselfish, needing a protective insistence on the rights she would never claim for herself. No one had ever treated her quite like that before. Milord had loved her, of course, and had guarded her always from trouble (milord who always had such beautiful manners with everyone), but he himself was so dominating a personality that other people fell naturally into his shadow. Her children loved her too, or so Genoux supposed, for it was unthinkable to Genoux that a child should not love its mother, even after the age of sixty, but there had been times when Genoux could not at all approve of their manner towards their mother; Lady Charlotte, for instance, was really too tyrannical, arriving at Elm Park Gardens at all hours of the day, her very aspect enough to make a timid old lady tremble. Very often one could detect a veiled impatience behind her words. And they were all too energetic, in Genoux's opinion, except for Lady Edith and Mr Kay; they bustled their poor mother about, talking loudly and taking it for granted that her powers were equal with their own. Once, when Lady Slane was going out with Mr William, she had proposed taking a taxi; but Mr William had said no, they could quite well go in a bus, and Genoux, who was holding the front door open for them, had nearly produced her purse to offer Mr William eighteen-pence. She wished now that she had indulged in that piece of irony. It was not reasonable to treat a lady of eighty-eight as though she were only sixty-five. Genoux, who herself was only two years younger than Lady Slane, waxed indignant when-ever she put on Lady Slane's galoshes in the hall of Elm Park Gardens and handed her an umbrella to go out into the rain. It was not right, especially when one considered the state Lady Slane had been accustomed to, sitting up on an elephant with a mahout behind her holding a parasol over her head. Genoux had preferred Calcutta to Elm Park Gardens.

But at Hampstead, thanks to Mr Bucktrout and Mr

Gosheron, the proper atmosphere had been at last achieved. It was modest; there were no aides-de-camp, no princes, but though modest it was warm, and affectionate, and respectful, and vigilant, and generous, just as it should be. Mr Bucktrout expressed himself in a style which Genoux thought extremely distinguished. He was odd, certainly, but he was a gentleman – un vrai monsieur. He had strange and beautiful ideas; he was never in a hurry; he would break off in the middle of business to talk about Descartes or the satisfying quality of pattern. And when he said pattern, he did not mean the pattern on a wallpaper; he meant the pattern of life. Mr Gosheron was never in a hurry either. Sometimes, by way of comment, he lifted his bowler hat at the back and scratched his head with his pencil. He spoke very little, and always in a low voice. He deplored the decay of craftsmanship in the modern world; refused to employ trades-union men, and had assembled a troop of workmen most of whom he had trained himself, and who were consequently so old that Genoux was sometimes afraid they would fall off their ladders. The workmen, too, had entered into the conspiracy to please Lady Slane; they greeted her arrival always with beaming smiles, took off their caps, and hastened to move the paint-pots out of her way. Yet for all this leisurely manner pervading the house, the work seemed to proceed quite fast, and there was always some little surprise prepared for Lady Slane every time she came up to Hampstead.

Mr Bucktrout even gave her little presents, though his delicacy restrained them to a nature so modest and inexpensive that she could accept them without embarrassment. Sometimes it was a plant for her garden, sometimes a vase of flowers set with a curious effect of brilliance on a window-sill in an empty room. He was compelled to set them on a window-sill, he explained, since there were as yet no tables or other furniture, but Lady Slane suspected that he really preferred the window-sill, where he could so dispose his gift that the rays of the sun would fall upon it at the very hour when he expected his tenant. She teased him sometimes by arriving half-an-hour late, but he was undefeated; and once a ring of wet three inches away betrayed him: seeing that she was late, he had gone upstairs again to shift his flowers along into the sun. Old age, thought Lady Slane, must surely content itself with very small pleasures, judging by the pleasure she experienced at this confirmation of her suspicions. Weary, enfeebled, ready to go, she still could amuse herself by playing a tiny game in miniature with Mr Bucktrout and Mr Gosheron, a sort of minuet stepped out to a fading music, artificial perhaps, yet symbolic of some reality she had never achieved with her own children. The artificiality lay in the manner, the reality in the heart which invented it. Courtesy ceased to be blankly artificial, when prompted by real esteem; it became, simply, one of the decent, veiling graces; a formula by which a profounder feeling might be conveyed.

They were too old, all three of them, to feel keenly; to compete and circumvent and score. They must fall back upon the old measure of the minuet, in which the gentleman's bow expressed all his appreciative gallantry towards women, and the lady's fan raised a breeze insufficient to flutter her hair. That was old age, when people knew everything so well that they could no longer afford to express it save in symbols. Those days were gone when feeling burst its bounds and poured hot from the foundry, when the heart seemed likely to split with complex and contradictory desires; now there was nothing left but a landscape in monochrome, the features identical but all the colours gone from them, and nothing but a gesture left in the place of speech.

Meanwhile Mr Bucktrout brought his little offerings, and Lady Slane liked them best when they took the form of flowers.

Mr Bucktrout, as she began to discover him, revealed many little talents, among which a gift for arranging a bunch was not the least. He would make daring and surprising combinations of colour and form, till the result was more like a still-life painting than like a bunch of living flowers, yet informed with a life that no paint could rival. Set upon their window-sill, luminous in the sun, more luminous for the bare boards and plaster surrounding them, their texture appeared lit from within rather than from without. Nor did his inventiveness ever falter, for this week he would produce a bunch as garish as a gipsy, all blue and purple and orange, but next week a bunch discreet as a pastel, all rose and grey with a dash of yellow, and some feathery spray lightly touched with cream. Lady Slane, who might have been a painter, could appreciate his effects. Mr Bucktrout was an artist, said Lady Slane; and even Genoux, who did not care for flowers in the house because they dropped their petals over tables, and eventually had to be thrown away, making a damp mess in the waste-paper basket, even Genoux commented one day that 'Monsieur aurait dû se faire floriste.'

Little by little, seeing that his efforts were appreciated, his offerings became more personal. The vase of flowers was supplemented by a bunch for Lady Slane to pin against her shoulder. The first occasion having given rise to a difficulty, because, searching under her laces and ruffles, anxious not to disappoint the old gentleman, she could discover no pin, he thereafter always provided a large black safety pin pushed securely through the silver paper wrapped round the stalks, and Lady Slane dutifully used it, though she had been presciently careful to bring one with her. Of such small, tacit, and mutual courtesies was their relationship compact.

One day she asked him why he took so much trouble on her behalf. Why had he made it his business to find Mr Gosheron for her, to supervise his estimates, to look into every detail of the work? That, surely, was not customary in an agent, even in an owner-agent? Mr Bucktrout instantly became very serious. 'I have been wondering, Lady Slane,' he said, 'whether you would ask me that question. I am glad that you should have asked it, for I am always in favour of letting the daylight into the thickets of misunderstanding. You are right: it is not customary. Let us say that I do it because I have very little else to do, and that so long as you do not object, I am grateful to you for affording me the occupation.'

'No,' said Lady Slane, shy but determined; 'that is not the reason. Why do you take my interests in this way? You see, Mr Bucktrout, not only do you control Mr Gosheron – who, as a matter of fact, needs less controlling than any tradesman I ever met – but from the first you have been anxious to spare me as much as possible. I may not be very well versed in practical matters,' she said with her charming smile, 'but I have seen enough of the world to realise that business is not usually conducted on your system. Besides, my daughter Charlotte ... well, never mind about my daughter Charlotte. The fact remains that I am puzzled, and also rather curious.'

'I should not like you to think me a simpleton, Lady Slane,' said Mr Bucktrout very gravely. He hesitated, as though wondering whether he should take her into his confidence, then went off with a rush on another little speech. 'I am not a simpleton,' he said, 'nor am I a childish old man. I dislike childishness and all such rubbish. I feel nothing but impatience with the people who pretend that the world is other than it is. The world, Lady Slane, is pitiably horrible. It is horrible because it is based upon competitive struggle – and really one does not know whether to call the basis of that struggle a convention or a necessity. Is it some extraordinary delusion, or is it a law of life? Is it perhaps an animal law from which civilisation may eventually free us? At present it seems to me, Lady Slane, that man has founded all his calculations upon a mathematical system fundamentally false. His sums work out right for his own purposes, because he has crammed and constrained his planet into accepting his premises. Judged by other laws, though the answers would remain correct, the premises would appear merely crazy; ingenious enough, but crazy. Perhaps some day a true civilisation may supervene and write a big W against all our answers. But we have a long road to travel yet – a long road to travel.' He shook his head, pointed his foot, and became sunk in his musings.

'Then you think,' said Lady Slane, seeing that she must recall him from his abstractions, 'that anyone who goes against this extraordinary delusion is helping civilisation on?'

'I do, Lady Slane; most certainly I do. But in a world as at present constituted, it is a luxury that only poets can afford, or people advanced in age. I assure you that when I first went into business, after I had resigned my commission, I was fierce. It is really the only word. Fierce. No one could get the better of me. And the more severe my conduct, the more respect I earned. Nothing earns respect so quickly as letting your fellows see that you are a match for them. Other methods may earn you respect in the long run, but for a short-cut there is nothing like setting a high valuation on yourself and forcing others to accept it. Modesty, moderation, consideration, nicety – no good; they don't pay. If you were to meet one of my earlier colleagues, Lady Slane, he would tell you that in my day I had been a regular Juggernaut.'

'And when did you give up these principles of ruthlessness, Mr Bucktrout?' asked Lady Slane.

'You do not suspect me of boasting, Lady Slane, do you?' asked Mr Bucktrout, eyeing her. 'I am telling you all this so that you should realise that *naïveté* is not my weakness. As I said, you must not be allowed to think me a simpleton. – When did I give up these principles? Well, I set a term upon them; I determined that at sixty-five business properly speaking should know me no more. On my sixty-fifth birthday – or, to put it more correctly, on my sixty-sixth – I woke a free man. For my practice had always been a discipline rather than an inclination.'

'But what about this house?' asked Lady Slane. 'You told me that for thirty years you had refused tenants if you didn't like them. Surely that was inclination, wasn't it? It could hardly be described as business?'

'Ah,' said Mr Bucktrout, putting his finger to his nose, 'you are too shrewd, Lady Slane; you have too good a memory. But don't be too hard on me: this house was always my one little patch of folly. Or, should I say, my one little patch of sanity? I like to be exact in my expressions. I see, Lady Slane, that you are something of a tease. I mean no impertinence. If ladies did not tease, we should be in danger of taking ourselves too seriously. I always had a fancy, you see, that I should like to end my days in this house, so naturally I did not wish its atmosphere contaminated by any unsympathetic influence. You may have noticed – of course you have noticed – that its atmosphere is curiously ripened and detached. I have preserved that atmosphere with the greatest care, for although one cannot create an atmosphere, one can at least safeguard it against disturbance.'

'But if you want to live here yourself – very well, die here yourself,' said Lady Slane, seeing that he had raised a hand and was about to correct her, 'why have you let it to me?'

'Oh,' said Mr Bucktrout easily and consolingly, 'your tenancy, Lady Slane, is not likely to interfere with my intentions.'

For courteous though he was, Mr Bucktrout in this respect remained firmly unsentimental, making no bones about the fact that Lady Slane would require the house for a short period only. Whenever he discouraged her from unnecessary expenditure, he did so on the grounds that it was scarcely worth her while.

When she mentioned central heating, he reminded her that she would spend but few winters, if any, in this her last abode. 'Though to be sure,' he added sympathetically, 'there is no reason why one should not be comfortable while one may.' Genoux, overhearing this remark, summoned her religion to the support of her indignation. 'Monsieur pense donc qu'il n'y a pas de radiateurs au paradis? Il se fait une idée bien mièvre d'un Bon Dieu peu up-to-date.' Still, Mr Bucktrout persisted in his idea that oil lamps would suffice to warm the rooms. He worked out the amount of gallons of paraffin they would consume in one winter, and balanced them against the cost of a furnace and pipes to pierce the walls. 'But, Mr Bucktrout,' said Lady Slane, not without malice, 'as owner and agent you ought to encourage me to put in central heating. Think how strongly it would appeal to your next tenant.' 'Lady Slane,' replied Mr Bucktrout, 'consideration of my next tenant remains in a separate compartment from consideration of my present tenant. That has always been my rule in life; and thanks to it I have always been able to keep my relationships distinct. I am a great believer in sharp outline. I dislike a fuzz. Most people fell into the error of making their whole life a fuzz, pleasing nobody, least of all themselves. Compromise is the very breath of negation. My principle has been, that it is better to please one person a great deal than to please a number of persons a little, no matter how much offence you give. I have given a great deal of offence in my life, but of not one offensive instance do I repent. I believe in taking the interest of the moment. Life is so transitory, Lady Slane, that one must grab it by the tail as it flies past. No good in thinking of yesterday or to-morrow. Yesterday is gone, and to-morrow problematical. Even to-day is precarious enough, God knows. Therefore I say unto you,' said Mr Bucktrout, relapsing into Biblical language and pointing his foot as though to point his words, 'do not put in central heating, for you know not how long you may live to enjoy it. My next tenant is welcome to warm himself in hell. I am here to advise you; and my advice is, buy an oil-lamp – several oil-lamps. They will warm you and see you out, however often you may have to renew the wicks.' He changed his foot, and frisked his coat-tails in a little perorative flourish. Mr Gosheron, rather embarrassed, tilted his hat.

This conviction of the transcience of her tenure arose, Lady Slane discovered, from two causes: Mr Bucktrout's estimate of her own age, and his prophetic views as to the imminent end of the world. He discoursed gravely on this subject, undeterred by the presence of Genoux and Mr Gosheron, who preferred to avoid such topics and wanted respectively to talk of linen-cupboards and distemper. Genoux's sheets must wait, and Mr Gosheron's little discs of colour, miniature full-moons, called Pompeian-red, Stone-grey, Olive-green, Shrimp-pink. Mr Bucktrout's attention was too closely engaged with eternity for linen-cupboards and distemper to catch him in more than a perfunctory interest. He could bear with them for five minutes; not longer. After that he would stick his sarcasm into Mr Gosheron, saying such things as that his yard-measure varied in length from room to room, according as it ran north and south, or east and west, and that Genoux's shelves could never be truly level, seeing that the whole universe was based upon a curve, all of which disconcerted Genoux and Mr Gosheron, but made Genoux respect Mr Bucktrout the more for his learning, and made Mr Gosheron's hat tilt nearly on to the tip of his nose. Mr Bucktrout, observing this confusion, enlarged with sadistic pleasure. He knew that he had an appreciative audience in Lady Slane, even while he kept his feet on the ground sufficiently for her protection. 'As you may know,' he said, standing in an unfinished room while painters suspended their brushes in order to listen, 'there are at least four theories presaging the end of the world. Flame, flood, frost, and collision. There are others, but they are so unscientific and so improbable as to be negligible. Then there are, of course, the prophetic numbers. In so far as I believe numbers to be a basic part of the eternal harmonies, I am a convinced Pythagorean. Numbers exist in the void; it is impossible to imagine the destruction of numbers, even though you imagine the destruction of the universe. I do not mean by this that I hold with such ingenuities as the great sacred number of the Babylonians, twelve million nine hundred and sixty thousand, as you remember, nor yet in such calculations as William Miller's, who, by a system of additions and deductions, decided that the world would end on March 21, 1843. No. I have worked out my own system, Lady Slane, and I can assure you that, though distressing, it is irrefutable. The great annihilation is close at hand.' Mr Bucktrout was launched; he tiptoed across to the wall, and very carefully wrote up PΩMH with a bit of chalk. A painter came after him, and as carefully obliterated it with his brush.

'Mais en attendant, miladi,' said Genoux, 'mes draps?'

Lady Slane had never taken so much pleasure in anybody's company. She had never been so happy as with her two old gentlemen. She had played her part among brilliant people, important people, she had accommodated herself to their conversation, and, during the years of her association with worldly affairs, she had learnt to put together the scattered bits of information which to her were so difficult to collate or even to remember; thus she was always reminded of the days of her girlhood, when vast gaps seemed to exist in her knowledge, and when she was at a loss to know what people meant when they referred to the Irish Question or the Woman's Movement, or to Free Trade and Protection, two especial stumbling-blocks between which she could never distinguish instinctively, although she had had them explained to her a dozen times. She had always taken an enormous amount of trouble to disguise her ignorance from Henry. In the end she had learnt to succeed quite well, and he would disburden himself of his political perplexities without the slightest suspicion that his wife had long since lost the basis of his argument. She was secretly and bitterly ashamed of her insufficiency. But what was to be done about it? She could not, no, she simply could not, remember why Mr Asquith disliked Mr Lloyd George, or what exactly were the aims of Labour, that new and alarming Party. The most that she could do was to conceal her ignorance, while she scrambled round frenziedly in her brain for some recollected scrap of associated information which would enable her to make some adequate reply. During their years in Paris she had suffered especially, for the cleverness of French conversation (which she greatly admired) always made her feel outwitted; and though she could sit listening for hours in rapture to the spitting pyrotechnics of epigram and summary, marvelling at the ability of other people to compress into a phrase some aspect of life which, to her, from its very importance, demanded a lifetime of reflection, yet her quiescent pleasure was always spoilt by the dread that at a given moment some guest in mistaken politeness would turn to her, throwing her the ball she would be unable to catch, saying, 'Et Madame l'Ambassadrice, qu'en pense-t-elle?' And though she knew that inwardly she had understood what they were saying far better than they had understood it themselves – for the conversation of the French always seemed to turn upon the subjects which interested her most deeply, and about which she felt that she really knew something, could she but have expressed it – she remained stupidly inarticulate, saying something non-committal or something that she did not in the least mean, conscious meanwhile that Henry, sitting by, must

73

be suffering wretchedly from the poor figure his wife cut. Yet, in private, he was apt to say, though rarely, that she was the most intelligent woman he knew because, although often inarticulate, she never made a foolish remark.

That these agonies should remain private to herself was her constant prayer; neither Henry nor the guests at her table must ever find her out. There were other allied weaknesses of which she was also ashamed, though in a slightly less degree: her inability, for instance, to write out a cheque correctly, putting the same amount in figures as in words, remembering to cross it, remembering to sign her name; her inability to understand what a debenture was, or the difference between ordinary and deferred stock; and as for that extraordinary menagerie of bulls, bears, stags, and contango, she might as well have found herself in a circus of wild animals. She supposed dutifully that these things were of major importance, since they were clearly the things which kept the world on the move; she supposed that party politics and war and industry, and a high birth-rate (which she had learned to call manpower), and competition and secret diplomacy and suspicion, were all part of a necessary game, necessary since the cleverest people she knew made it their business, though to her, as a game, unintelligible; she supposed it must be so, though the feeling more frequently seized her of watching figures moving in the delusion of a terrible and ridiculous dream. The whole tragic system seemed to be based upon an extraordinary convention, as incomprehensible as the theory of money, which (so she had been told) bore no relation to the actual supply of gold. It was chance which had made men turn gold into their symbol, rather than stones; it was chance which had made men turn strife into their principle, rather than amity. That the planet might have got on better with stones and amity – a simple solution – had apparently never occurred to its inhabitants.

Her own children, do what she might, had grown up in the same traditions. Naturally. There they were, trying and striving, not content merely to *be*. Herbert, so sententious always, so ambitious in his stupid way; Carrie with her committees and her harsh managing voice, interfering with people who did not want to be interfered with, all for the love of interference, her mother felt sure; Charles with his perpetual grievances; William and Lavinia, always scraping and saving and paring, an occupation in itself. There was no true kindliness, no grace, no privacy in any of them. For Edith and Kay alone their mother could feel some sympathy: Edith, always in a muddle, trying to get things straight and only getting them more tangled, trying to stand back and take a look at life, the whole of it, an impossibility accepted by most people, but which really bothered Edith and made her unhappy (still, the uneasiness did her credit); Kay – well, of all her children, perhaps Kay, messing about among his compasses and astrolabes, was the one who strove and struggled least; the one who had, without knowing it, the strongest sense of his own entity, when he shut his door behind him and took out his duster to potter with it along the alignment of his shelves. Yes, Kay and Edith were nearest to her; that would be one of the secrets, one of the jokes, she would take away with her into the grave.

For the rest, she had been a lonely woman, always at variance with the creeds to which she apparently conformed. Every now and then she had known some delicious encounter with a spirit attuned to her own. There had been the young man who accompanied them to Fatihpur Sikhri; a young man whose name she had forgotten, or had never known; but into whose eyes she had looked for one moment, and then, disturbed, had dismissed by her very gesture of strolling off to rejoin the Viceroy and his group of sun-helmeted officials. Such encounters had been rare, and, thanks to the circumstances of her life, brief. (She retained, however, a conviction that many spirits were fundamentally attuned, but so thickly overlaid by the formulas of the world that the clear requisite note could no longer be struck.) With Mr Bucktrout and Mr Gosheron she found herself entirely at ease. She could tell Mr Bucktrout without embarrassment that she was unable to distinguish rates from taxes. She could tell Mr Gosheron that she was unable to distinguish between a volt and an ampère. Neither of them tried to explain. They gave up at once, and simply said, leave it to me. She left it, and knew that her trust would not be misplaced.

Strange, the relief and release that this companionship brought her! Was it due to the weariness of old age, or to the long-awaited return to childhood, when all decisions and responsibilities might again be left in the hands of others, and one might be free to dream in a world of whose sunshine and benignity one was convinced? And she thought, if only I were young once more I would stand for all that was calm and contemplative, opposed to the active, the scheming, the striving, the false – yes! the false, she exclaimed, striking her fist into the palm of the other hand with unaccustomed energy; and then, trying to correct herself, she wondered whether this were not merely a negative creed, a negation of life; perhaps even a confession of insufficient vitality; and came to the conclusion that it was not so, for in contemplation (and also in the pursuit of the one chosen avocation which she had had to renounce) she could pierce to a happier life more truly than her children who reckoned things by their results and activities.

She remembered how, crossing the Persian desert with Henry, their cart had been escorted by flocks of butterflies, white and yellow, which danced on either side and overhead and all around them, now flying ahead in a concerted movement, now returning to accompany them, amused as it were to restrain their swift frivolity to a flitting round this lumbering conveyance, but still unable to suit their pace to such sobriety, so, to relieve their impatience, soaring up into the air or dipping between the very axles, coming out on the other side before the horses had had time to put down another hoof; making, all the while, little smuts of shadow on the sand, like little black anchors dropped, tethering them by invisible cables to earth, but dragged about with the same capricious swiftness, obliged to follow; and she remembered thinking, lulled by the monotonous progression that trailed after the sun from dawn to dusk, like a plough that should pursue the sun in one straight slow furrow round and round the world – she remembered thinking that this was something like her own life, following Henry Holland like the sun, but every now and then moving into a cloud of butterflies which were her own irreverent, irrelevant thoughts, darting and dancing, but altering the pace of the progression not by one tittle; never brushing the carriage with their wings; flickering always, and evading; sometimes rushing on ahead, but returning again to tease and to show off, darting between the axles; having an independent and a lovely life; a flock of ragamuffins skimming above the surface of the desert and around the trundling waggon; but Henry, who was travelling on a tour of investigation, could only say, 'Terrible, the ophthalmia among these people – I must really do something about it,' and, knowing that he was right and would speak to the missionaries, she had withdrawn her attention from the butterflies and had transferred it to her duty, determining that when they reached Yezd or Shiraz, or wherever it might be, she also would take the missionaries' wives to task about the ophthalmia in the villages and would make arrangements for a further supply of boracic to be sent out from England.

But, perversely, the flittering of the butterflies had always remained more important.

PART TWO

Her heart sat silent through the noise
And concourse of the street;
There was no hurry in her hands,
No hurry in her feet.

CHRISTINA ROSSETTI

Sitting there in the sun at Hampstead, in the late summer, under the south wall and the ripened peaches, doing nothing with her hands, she remembered the day she had become engaged to Henry. She had plenty of leisure now, day in, day out, to survey her life as a tract of country traversed, and at last become a landscape instead of separate fields or separate years and days, so that it became a unity and she could see the whole view, and could even pick out a particular field and wander round it again in spirit, though seeing it all the while as it were from a height, fallen into its proper place, with the exact pattern drawn round it by the hedge, and the next field into which the gap in the hedge would lead. So, she thought, could she at last put circles round her life. Slowly she crossed that day, as one crosses a field by a little path through the grasses, with the sorrel and the buttercups waving on either side; she crossed it again slowly, from breakfast to bed-time, and each hour, as one hand of the clock passed over the other, regained for her its separate character: this was the hour, she thought, when I first came downstairs that day, swinging my hat by its ribbons; and this was the hour when he persuaded me into the garden, and sat with me on the seat beside the lake, and told me it was not true that with one blow of its wing a swan could break the leg of a man. She had listened to him, paying dutiful attention to the swan which had actually drifted up to them by the bank, dipping its beak and then curving to probe irritably into the snowy tuft of feathers on its breast; but she was thinking less of the swan than of the young whiskers on Henry's cheek, only her

81

thoughts had merged, so that she wondered whether Henry's brown curls were as soft as the feathers on the breast of the swan, and all but reached out an idle hand to feel them. Then he passed from the swan, as though that had been but a gambit to cover his hesitation, and the next thing she knew was that he was speaking earnestly, bending forward and even fingering a flounce of her dress, as though anxious, although unaware of his anxiety, to establish some kind of contact between himself and her; but for her all true contact had been severed from the moment he began to speak so earnestly, and she felt no longer even the slight tug of desire to put out her hand and touch the curly whiskers on his cheek. Those words which he must utter so earnestly, in order that his tone might carry their full weight; those words which he seemed to produce from some serious and secret place, hauling them up from the bottom of the well of his personality; those words which belonged to the region of weighty and adult things – those words removed him from her more rapidly than an eagle catching him up in its talons to the sky. He had gone. He had left her. Even while she conscientiously gazed at him and listened, she knew that he was already miles and miles away. He had passed into the sphere where people marry, beget and bear children, bring them up, give orders to servants, pay income-tax, understand about dividends, speak mysteriously in the presence of the young, take decisions for themselves, eat what they like, and go to bed at the hour which pleases them. Mr Holland was asking her to accompany him into that sphere. He was asking her to be his wife.

It was clearly impossible, to her mind, that she should accept. The idea was preposterous. She could not possibly follow Mr Holland into that sphere; could follow him, perhaps, less than any man, for she knew him to be very brilliant, and marked out for that most remote and impressive of mysteries, a Career. She had heard her father say that young Holland would be Viceroy of India before they had heard the last of him. That would mean that she must be Vicereine, and at the thought she had turned upon him the glance of a startled fawn. Instantly interpreting that glance according to his desires, Mr Holland had clasped her in his arms and had kissed her with ardour but with restraint upon the lips.

What was a poor girl to do? Before she well knew what was happening, there was her mother smiling through tears, her father putting his hand on Mr Holland's shoulder, her sisters asking if they might all be bridesmaids, and Mr Holland himself standing very upright, very proud, very silent, smiling a little, bowing, and looking at her with an expression that even her inexperience could define only as proprietary. In a trice, like that, she had been changed from the person she was into somebody completely different. Or had she not? She could not detect any metamorphosis as having taken place within herself to match the sudden crop of smiles on all those faces. She certainly felt the same as before. A sense of terror possessed her over the novelty of her opinion being sought on any matter, and she hastily restored the decision into the hands of others. By this method she felt that she might delay the moment when she must definitely and irrevocably become that other person. She could go on, for a little, secretly continuing to be herself.

And what, precisely, had been herself, she wondered – an old woman looking back on the girl she once had been? This wondering was the softest, most wistful, of occupations; yet it was not melancholy; it was, rather, the last, supreme luxury; a luxury she had waited all her life to indulge. There was just time, in this reprieve before death, to indulge herself to the full. She had, after all, nothing else to do. For the first time in her life – no, for the first time since her marriage – she had nothing else to do. She could lie back against death and examine life. Meanwhile, the air was full of the sound of bees.

She saw herself as a young girl walking beside the lake. She walked slowly, swinging her hat; she walked meditatively, her eyes cast down, and as she walked she prodded the tip of her parasol into the spongy earth. She wore the flounced and feminine muslins of 1860. Her hair was ringleted, and one ringlet escaped and fell softly against her neck. A curly spaniel accompanied her, snuffling into the bushes. They had all the appearance of a girl and a dog in an engraving from some sentimental keepsake. Yes, that was she, Deborah Lee, not Deborah Holland, not Deborah Slane; the old woman closed her eyes, the better to hold the vision. The girl walking beside the lake was unaware, but the old woman beheld the whole of adolescence, as who should catch a petal in the act of unfolding; dewy, wavering, virginal, eager, blown by generous yet shy impulses, as timid as a leveret and as swift, as confiding as a doe peeping between the tree trunks, as light-foot as a dancer waiting in the wings, as soft and scented as a damask rose, as full of laughter as a fountain – yes, that was youth, hesitant as one upon an unknown threshold, yet ready to run her breast against a spear. The old woman looked closer; she saw the tender flesh, the fragile curves, the deep and glistening eyes, the untried mouth, the ringless hands; and, loving the girl that she had been, she tried to catch some tone of her voice, but the girl remained silent, walking as though behind a wall of glass. She was alone. That meditative solitude seemed a part of her very essence. Whatever else might be in her head, it was certain that neither love, nor romance, nor any of the emotions usually ascribed to the young, were in it. If she dreamed, it was of no young Adam. And there again, thought Lady Slane, one should not wrong the young by circumscribing them with one sole set of notions, for youth is richer than that; youth is full of hopes reaching out, youth will burn the river and set all the belfries of the world ringing; there is not only love to be considered, there are also such things as fame and achievement and genius – which might be in one's heart, knocking against one's ribs, who knows? let us retire quickly to a turret, and see if the genius within one will not declare itself. But, dear me, thought Lady Slane, it was a poor look-out in eighteen-sixty for a girl to think of fame.

For Lady Slane was in the fortunate position of seeing into the heart of the girl who had been herself. She could mark not only the lingering step, the pause, the frowning brows, the prod of the parasol into the earth, the broken reflection quivering down into the waters of the lake; she could read also into the thoughts which accompanied this solitary ramble. She could make herself a party to their secrecy and their extravagance. For the thoughts which ran behind this delicate and maidenly exterior were of an extravagance to do credit even to a wild young man. They were thoughts of nothing less than escape and disguise; a changed name, a travestied sex, and freedom in some foreign city – schemes on a par with the schemes of a boy about to run away to sea. Those ringlets would drop beneath the scissors – and here a hand stole upward, as though prophetically to caress a shorn sleek head; that fichu would be replaced by a shirt – and here the fingers felt for the knot of a tie; those skirts would be kicked for ever aside – and here, very shyly this time, the hand dropped towards the opening of a trouser pocket. The image of the girl faded, and in its place stood a slender boy. He was a boy, but essentially he was a sexless creature, a mere symbol and emanation of youth, one who had forsworn for ever the delights and rights of sex to serve what seemed to his rioting imagination a nobler aim. Deborah, in short, at the age of seventeen, had determined to become a painter.

The sun, which had been warming her old bones and the peaches on the wall, crept westering behind a house so that she shivered slightly, and, rising, dragged her chair forward on to the still sunlit grass. She would follow that bygone ambition from its dubious birth, through the months when it steadied and increased and coursed like blood through her, to the days when it languished and lost heart, for all her efforts to keep it alive. She saw it now for what it was: the only thing of value that had entered her life. Reality she had had in plenty, or what with other women passed for reality – but she could not go into those realities now, she must attach herself to that transcending reality for as long as she could hold it, it was so firm, it made her so happy even to remember how it had once sustained her; for she was not merely telling herself about it now, but feeling it again, right down in some deep place; it had the pervading nature of love while love is strong, unlike the cold recital of love in reminiscence. She burned again with the same ecstasy, the same exaltation. How fine it had been, to live in that state of rapture! how fine, how difficult, how supremely worth while! A nun in her novitiate was not more vigilant than she. Drawn tight as a firm wire, she had trembled then to a touch; she had been poised as a young god in the integrity of creation. Images clustered in her mind, but every image must be of a nature extravagantly lyrical. Nothing else would fit. A crimson cloak, a silver sword, were neither sumptuous enough nor pure enough to express the ardours of that temper. By God, she exclaimed, the young blood running again generously through her, that is a life worth living! The life of the artist, the creator, looking closely, feeling widely; detail and horizon included in the same sweep of the glance. And she remembered how the shadow on the wall was a greater delight to her than the thing itself, and how she had looked at a stormy sky, or at a tulip in the sun, and, narrowing her eyes, had forced those things into relation with everything that made a pattern in her mind.

So for months she had lived intensely, secretly, building herself in preparation, though she never laid brush to canvas, and only dreamed herself away into the far future. She could gauge the idleness of ordinary life by the sagging of her spirits whenever the flame momentarily burnt lower. Those glimpses of futility alarmed her beyond all reason. The flame had gone out, she thought in terror, every time it drooped; it would never revive; she must be left cold and unillumined. She could never learn that it would return, as the great garland of rhythm swept once more upwards and the light poured over her, warm as the reappearing sun, incandescent as a star, and on wings she rose again, steadying in their flight. It was thus a life of extremes that she lived, at one moment rapt, at another moment sunk in despondency. But of all this not one flicker mounted to the surface.

Some instinct, perhaps, warned her to impart her unsuitable secret to none, knowing very well that her parents, indulgent indeed, but limited, as was natural, would receive her declaration with a smile and a pat on the head, and an interchanged glance passing between themselves, saying as plainly as possible, 'That's our pretty bird! and the first personable young man who comes along will soon put these notions to rout.' Or, perhaps, it was merely the treasured privacy of the artist which kept her silent. She was as docile as could be. She would run errands in the house for her mother, strip the lavender into a great cloth, make bags for it to lie between the sheets, write labels for the pots of jam, brush the pug, and fetch her cross-stitch after dinner without being bidden. Acquaintances envied her parents their eldest daughter. There were many who already had an eye on her as a wife for their son. But a thread of ambition was said to run through the modest and ordered household, a single thread, for Deborah's parents, arrived at middle age with their quiver-full of sons and daughters, preferred their easy rural domesticity to any worldly advantage, but for Deborah their aims were different: Deborah must be the wife of a good man, certainly, but if also the wife of a man to whose career she might be a help and an ornament – why, then, so much the better. Of this, naturally, nothing was said to Deborah. It would not do to turn the child's head.

Lady Slane rose again and drew her chair a little farther forward into the sun, for the shadow was beginning to creep, chilling her.

Her eldest brother had been away, she remembered; he was twenty-three; he had left home, as young men do; he had gone out into the world. She wondered sometimes what young men did, out in the world; she imagined them laughing and ruffling; going here and there, freely; striding home through the empty streets at dawn, or hailing a hansom and driving off to Richmond. They talked with strangers; they entered shops; they frequented the theatres. They had a club – several clubs. They were accosted by importunate women in the shadows, and could take their bodies for a night into their thoughtless embrace. Whatever they did, they did with a fine carelessness, a fine freedom, and when they came home they need give no account of their doings; moreover, there was an air of freemasonry among men, based upon their common liberty, very different from the freemasonry among women, which was always prying and personal and somehow a trifle obscene. But if the difference between her lot and her brother's occurred to Deborah, she said nothing of it. Beside the spaciousness of his opportunity and experience, she might justifiably feel a little cramped. If he, choosing to read for the Bar, were commended and applauded in his choice, why should she, choosing to be a painter, so shrink from announcing her decision that she was driven to secret and desperate plans for travesty and flight? There was surely a discrepancy somewhere. But everybody seemed agreed – so well agreed, that the matter was not even discussed: there was only one employment open to women.

The solidity of this agreement was brought home to Deborah from the moment that Mr Holland led her to her mother from the lake. She had been a favourite child, but never had the rays of approval beaten down so warmly upon her. She was put in mind of those Italian pictures, showing heaven opened and the Eternal Father beaming down between golden rays like the sticks of a fan, so that one stretched out one's fingers to warm them at the glow of his benignity, as at the bars of a fire. So now with Deborah and her parents, not to mention the rest of her world, she was made to feel that in becoming engaged to Mr Holland she had performed an act of exceeding though joyful virtue, had in fact done that which had always been expected of her; had fulfilled herself, besides giving enormous satisfaction to other people. She found herself suddenly surrounded by a host of assumptions. It was assumed that she trembled for joy in his presence, languished in his absence, existed solely (but humbly) for the furtherance of his ambitions, and thought him the most remarkable man alive, as she herself was the most favoured of women, a belief in which everybody was fondly prepared to indulge her. Such was the unanimity of these assumptions that she was almost persuaded into believing them true.

This was all very well, and for some days she allowed herself a little game of make-believe, imagining that she would be able to extricate herself without too much difficulty, for she was but eighteen, and it is pleasant to be praised, especially by those of whom one stands in affectionate awe; but presently she perceived that innumerable little strands like the thread of a spider were fastening themselves round her wrists and ankles, and that each one of them ran up to its other end in somebody's heart. There was her father's heart, and Mr Holland's – whom she had learnt to call, but not very readily, Henry – and as for her mother's heart, that might have been a railway terminus, so many shining threads ran up into it out of sight – threads of pride and love and relief and maternal agitation and feminine welcome of fuss. Deborah stood there, bound and perplexed, and wondering what she should do next. Meanwhile, as she stood, feeling as silly as a May-queen with the streamers winding round her, she discerned upon the horizon people arriving with gifts, all converging upon her, as vassals bearing tribute: Henry with a ring – and the placing of it upon her finger was a real ceremony; her sisters with a dressing-bag they had clubbed together to buy; and then her mother with enough linen to rig a wind-jammer: table-cloths, dinner-napkins, towels (hand and bath), tea-cloths, kitchen rubbers, pantry cloths, dusters, and, of course, sheets, which when displayed proved to be double, and all embroidered with a monogram, not at first sight decipherable, but which on closer inspection Deborah disentangled into the letters D.H. After that, she was lost. She was lost into the foam and billows of silks, satins, poplins, and alpacas, while women knelt and crawled around her with their mouths full of pins, and she herself was made to stand, and turn, and bend her arm, and straighten it again, and was told to step out carefully, while the skirt made a ring on the floor, and was told that she must bear having her stays pulled a little tighter, for the lining had been cut a shade too small. It seemed to her then that she was always tired, and that people showed their love for her by making her more tired than she already was, by piling up her obligations and dancing round her until she knew not whether she stood still or spun round like a top; and time also seemed to have entered into the conspiracy, maliciously shortening the days, so that they rushed her along and were no more than a snowstorm of notes and tissue paper and of white roses that came every day from the florist by Henry's order. Yet all the time, as an undercurrent, the older women seemed to have a kind of secret among themselves, a reason for sage smiles and glances, a secret whereby something of Deborah's strength must be saved from this sweet turmoil and stored up for some greater demand that would be put upon her.

Indeed, these weeks before the wedding were dedicated wholly to the rites of a mysterious feminism. Never, Deborah thought, had she been surrounded by so many women. Matriarchy ruled. Men might have dwindled into insignificance on the planet. Even Henry himself did not count for much. (Yet he was there, terribly there, in the background; and thus, she thought, might a Theban mother have tired her daughter before sending her off to the Minotaur.) Women appeared from all quarters: aunts, cousins, friends, dressmakers, corsetières, milliners, and even a young French maid, whom Deborah was to have for her own, and who regarded her new mistress with wondering eyes, as one upon whom the gods had set their seal. In these rites Deborah – another assumption – was expected to play a most complicated part. She was expected to know what it was all about, and yet the core of the mystery was to remain hidden from her. She was to be the recipient of smiling congratulations, yet also she must be addressed as 'My little Deborah!' an exclamation from which she suspected that the adjective 'poor' was missing just by chance, and clipped in long embraces, almost valedictory in their benevolence. Oh, what a pother, she thought, women make about marriage! and yet who can blame them, she added, when one recollects that marriage – and its consequences – is the only thing that women have to make a pother about in the whole of their lives? Though the excitement be vicarious, it will do just as well. Is it not for this function that they have been formed, dressed, bedizened, educated – if so one-sided an affair may be called education – safeguarded, kept in the dark, hinted at, segregated, repressed, all that at a given moment they may be delivered, or may deliver their daughters over, to Minister to a Man?

But how on earth she was going to minister to him, Deborah

did not know. She knew only that she remained completely alien to all this fuss about the wonderful opportunity which was to be hers. She supposed that she was not in love with Henry, but, even had she been in love with him, she could see therein no reason for foregoing the whole of her own separate existence. Henry was in love with her, but no one proposed that he should forego his. On the contrary, it appeared that in acquiring her he was merely adding something extra to it. He would continue to lunch with his friends, travel down to his constituency, and spend his evenings at the House of Commons; he would continue to enjoy his free, varied, and masculine life, with no ring upon his finger or difference in his name to indicate the change in his estate; but whenever he felt inclined to come home she must be there, ready to lay down her book, her paper, or her letters; she must be prepared to listen to whatever he had to say; she must entertain his political acquaintances; and even if he beckoned her across the world she must follow. Well, she thought, that recalled Ruth and Boaz and was very pleasant for Henry. No doubt he would do his part by her, as he understood it. Sitting down by her, as her needle plucked in and out of her embroidery, he would gaze fondly at her bent head, and would say he was lucky to have such a pretty little wife to come back to. For all his grandeur as a Cabinet Minister, he would say it like any middle-class or working-man husband. And she ought to look up, rewarded. For all his grandeur and desirability as Governor or Viceroy, he would disregard the blandishments of women ambitious for their husbands, beyond the necessary gallantries of social intercourse, and would be faithful to her, so that the green snake of jealousy would never slip across her path. He would advance in honours, and with a genuine pride would see a coronet appear on the head of the little black shadow which had doubled him for so many years. But where, in such a programme, was there room for a studio?

It would not do if Henry were to return one evening and be met by a locked door. It would not do if Henry, short of ink or blotting-paper, were to emerge irritably only to be told that Mrs Holland was engaged with a model. It would not do if Henry were appointed governor to some distant colony, to tell him that the drawing-master unfortunately lived in London. It would not do, if Henry wanted another son, to tell him that she had just embarked on a special course of study. It would not do, in such a world of assumptions, to assume that she had equal rights with Henry. For such privileges marriage was not ordained.

But for certain privileges marriage had been ordained, and going to her bedroom Deborah took out her prayer-book and turned up the Marriage Service. It was ordained for the procreation of children – well, she knew that; one of her friends had told her, before she had time to stop her ears. It was ordained so that women might be loving and amiable, faithful and obedient to their husbands, holy and godly matrons in all quietness, sobriety, and peace. All this no doubt was, to a certain extent, parliamentary language. But still it bore a certain relation to fact. And still she asked, where, in this system, was there room for a studio?

Henry, always charming and courteous, and now very much in love, smiled most indulgently when she finally brought herself to ask him if he would object to her painting after they were married. Object! of course he would not object. He thought an elegant accomplishment most becoming in a woman. 'I confess,' he said, 'that of all feminine accomplishments the piano is my favourite, but since your talent lies in another direction, my dearest, why then we'll make the best of it.' And he went on to say how pleasant it would be for them both if she kept a record of their travels, and mentioned something about water-colour sketches in an album, which they could show their friends at home. But when Deborah said that that was not quite what she had in mind – she had thought of something more serious, she said, though her heart was in her mouth as she said it – he had smiled again, more fondly and indulgently than ever, and had said there would be plenty of time to see about that, but for his own part, he fancied that after marriage she would find plenty of other occupations to help her pass the days.

Then, indeed, she felt trapped and wild. She knew very well what he meant. She hated him for his Jovian detachment and superiority, for his fond but nevertheless smug assumptions, for his easy kindliness, and most of all for the impossibility of blaming him. He was not to blame. He had only taken for granted the things he was entitled to take for granted, thereby ranging himself with the women and entering into the general conspiracy to defraud her of her chosen life.

She was very childish, very tentative, very uncertain, very unaware. But at least she did recognise that the conversation had been momentous. She had her answer. She never referred to it again.

Yet she was no feminist. She was too wise a woman to indulge in such luxuries as an imagined martyrdom. The rift between herself and life was not the rift between man and woman, but the rift between the worker and the dreamer. That she was a woman, and Henry a man, was really a matter of chance. She would go no further than to acknowledge that the fact of her being a woman made the situation a degree more difficult.

Lady Slane dragged her chair this time half-way down the little garden. Genoux saw her from the windows and came out with a rug, 'pour m'assurer que miladi ne prendra pas froid. Que dirait ce pauvre milord, s'il pensait que miladi prenait froid? Lui, qui toujours avait tant de soin de miladi!'

Yes, she had married Henry, and Henry had always been

extremely solicitous that she should not catch cold. He had taken the greatest possible care of her; she might say with truth that she had always led a sheltered life. (But was that what she had wanted?) Whether in England, or in Africa, or in Australia, or in India, Henry had always seen to it that she had the least possible amount of trouble. Perhaps that was his way of compensating her for the independence she had foregone for his sake. Perhaps Henry – an odd thought! – had realised more than his convenience would ever allow him to admit. Perhaps he had consciously or unconsciously tried to smother her longings under a pack of rugs and cushions, like putting a broken heart to sleep on a feather bed. She had always been surrounded by servants, secretaries, and aides-de-camp, fulfilling the function of those little fenders which prevent a ship from bumping too roughly against the quay. Usually, indeed, they had exceeded their duties, from sheer devotion to Lady Slane, from a sheer wish to protect and spare her, who was so gentle, so plucky, so self-effacing, and so feminine. Her fragility aroused the chivalry of men, her modesty precluded the antagonism of women, her spirit awoke the respect of both. And as for Henry himself, though he liked to dally with pretty and sycophantic women, bending over them in a way which often gave Lady Slane a pang, he had never thought another woman in the world worthy to compare.

Wrapped in the rug which in a sense had been put round her knees by Henry, she wondered now how close had ever been the communion between them? The coldness with which she was now able to estimate their relationship frightened her a little, yet it took her back in some curious way to the days when she had plotted to elude her parents and consecrate herself to an existence which, although conventionally reprehensible, should, essentially, be dedicated to the most severe and difficult integrity. *Then*, she had been face to face with life, and that had seemed a reason for a necessity for the clearest thinking; *now*, she was face to face with death, and that again seemed a reason for the truest possible estimate of values, without evasion. The middle period alone had been confused.

Confused. Other people would not think it confused. Other people would point to their marriage as a perfect marriage; to herself and Henry, severally, as the perfect wife and husband. They would say that neither had ever 'looked at' anybody else. They would envy them, as the partners in an honourable career and the founders of a satisfactory and promising dynasty. They would commiserate now with her in being left alone; but they would reflect that, after all, an old woman of eighty-eight who had had her life was not so much to be pitied, and might spend her remaining years in looking forward to the day when her husband – young once more, garlanded with flowers, and robed in some kind of night-gown – would stand waiting to greet her on the Other Side. They would say she had been happy.

But what was happiness? Had she been happy? That was a strange, clicking word to have coined – meaning something definite to the whole English-speaking race – a strange clicking word with its short vowel and its spitting double p's, and its pert tip-tilted y at the end, to express in two syllables a whole summary of life. Happy. But one was happy at one moment, unhappy two minutes later, and neither for any good reason; so what did it mean? It meant, if it meant anything at all, that some uneasy desire wanted black to be black, and white, white; it meant that in the jungle of the terrors of life, the tiny creeping creatures sought reassurance in a formula. Certainly, there had been moments of which one could say: *Then*, I was happy; and with greater certainty: *Then*, I was unhappy – when little Robert had lain in his coffin, for instance, strewn with rose-petals by his sobbing Syrian nurse – but whole regions had intervened, which were just existence. Absurd to ask of those, had she been happy or unhappy? It seemed merely as though someone were asking a question about someone that was not herself, clothing the question in a word that bore no relation to the shifting, elusive, iridescent play of life; trying to do something impossible, in fact, like compressing the waters of a lake into a tight, hard ball. Life was that lake, thought Lady Slane, sitting under the warm south wall amid the smell of the peaches; a lake offering its even surface to many reflections, gilded by the sun, silvered by the moon, darkened by a cloud, roughened by a ripple; but level always, a plane, keeping its bounds, not to be rolled up into a tight, hard ball, small enough to be held in the hand, which was what people were trying to do when they asked if one's life had been happy or unhappy.

No, that was not the question to ask her – not the question to ask anybody. Things were not so simple as all that. Had they asked her whether she had loved her husband, she could have answered without hesitation: yes, she had loved him. There had been no moments when she could differentiate and say: *Then*, at such a moment, I loved him; and again, *Then*, at such another, I loved him not. The stress had been constant. Her love for him had been a straight black line drawn right through her life. It had hurt her, it had damaged her, it had diminished her, but she had been unable to curve away from it. All the parts of her that were not Henry Holland's had pulled in opposition, yet by this single giant of love they had all been pulled over, as the weaker team in a tug-of-war. Her ambitions, her secret existence, all had given way. She had loved him so much, that even her resentment was subdued. She could not grudge him even the sacrifice he had imposed upon her. Yet she was not one of those women whose gladness in sacrifice is such that the sacrifice ceases to be a sacrifice. Her own youthful visions had been incompatible with such a love, and in giving them up she knew that she gave up something of incomparable value.

That was what she had done for Henry Holland, and Henry Holland had never known it.

At last, she could see him and herself in retrospect; more precious than that, she could bear to examine him without disloyalty. She could bear to shed the frenzied loyalty of the past. Not that the anguish of her love had faded from her memory. She could still remember the days when she had prayed for the safety and happiness of Henry Holland, superstitiously, to a God in whom she had never wholly believed. Childish and ardent, the words of her prayer had grown, fitting themselves to her necessity. 'O Lord,' she had prayed nightly, 'take care of my beloved Henry, make him happy, keep him safe, O Lord, from all dangers, whether of illness or accident, preserve him for me who love him better than anything in heaven or earth.' Thus she had prayed; and as she prayed, every night, the words renewed their sharpness; whenever she whispered 'safe from all dangers, whether of illness or accident,' she had seen Henry knocked down by a dray, Henry breathing in pneumonia, as though either disaster were actually present; and when she whispered 'me who love him better than anything in heaven or earth,' she had undergone the nightly anxiety of wondering whether the inclusion of heaven were not blasphemous and might not offend a jealous God, for surely it was fringing on blasphemy to flaunt Henry as dearer to her than anything in earth or heaven – which involved God Himself, the very God she would propitiate – a blasphemy which might strike deeper than her intended appeal? Yet she persisted in her prayer, for it was strictly up against the truth. Henry was dearer, far dearer, to her than anything else in heaven or earth. He had decoyed her even into holding him dearer than her own ambition. She could not say otherwise, to a God who (if He existed at all) would certainly know her heart whether she whispered it out in prayer or not. Therefore, she might as well give herself the nightly luxury of whispering the truth, heard of God, she hoped; unheard, she hoped, of Henry Holland. It was a comfort to her. After her prayer, she could sleep, having ensured safety for Henry for at least twenty-four hours, the limit she set upon the efficacy of her prayer. And Henry Holland, she remembered, had been a difficult and dangerous treasure to preserve, even with the support of secret intercession. His career had been so active, so detached from the sheltered life of her petitions! She, who would have chosen for him the methodical existence of a Dutch bulb-grower, a mynheer concerned with nothing more disturbing than the fertilisation of a new tulip, while the doves in their wicker cage cooed and spread their wings in the sun, she had seen him always in a processional life, threatened by bombs, riding on an elephant through Indian cities, shut away from her by ceremony or business; and when physical danger was temporarily suspended in some safe capital, London, Paris, or Washington – when, great servant of the State, he found employment at home or travelled abroad on some peaceful mission – then other demands were made upon her watchfulness: she must be swift to detect his need for re-assurance when a momentary discouragement overcame him; when, mooning, he strayed up to her and drooped over her chair, saying nothing, but waiting (as she knew) for some soft protection to come from her and fold itself around him like a cloak, yet it must all be done without a word directly spoken; she must restore his belief that the obstructiveness of his Government or the opposition of his rivals was due to their short-sightedness or envy, and to no deficiency within himself, yet must not allow him to know that she guessed at his mood of self-mistrust or the whole fabric of her comfort would be undone. And when she had accomplished this feat, this reconstruction of extreme delicacy and extreme solidity – when he left her, to go back strengthened to his business – then, with her hands lying limp, symbol of her exhaustion, and a sweet emptiness within her, as though her self had drained away to flow into the veins of another person – then, sinking, drowning, she wondered whether she had not secretly touched the heights of rapture.

Yet even this, the statement of her love and the recollection of its more subtle demands, failed to satisfy her in its broad simplification. The statement that she had loved, though indisputable, still admitted of infinite complexity. Who was the she, the 'I,' that had loved? And Henry, who and what was he? A physical presence, threatened by time and death, and therefore the dearer for that factual menace? Or was his physical presence merely the palpable projection, the symbol, of something which might justly be called himself? Hidden away under the symbol of their corporeality, both in him and in her, doubtless lurked something which was themselves. But that self was hard to get at; obscured by the too familiar trappings of voice, name, appearance, occupation, circumstance, even the fleeting perception of self became blunted or confused. And there were many selves. She could never be the same self with him as when she was alone; and even that solitary self which she pursued, shifted, changed, melted away as she approached it, she could never drive it into a dark corner, and there, like a robber in the night, hold it by the throat against the wall, the hard core of self chased into a blind alley of refuge. The very words which clothed her thoughts were but another falsification; no word could stand alone, like a column of stone or the trunk of a tree, but must riot instantly into a tropical tangle of associations; the fact, it seemed, was as elusive and as luxuriant as the self. Only in a wordless trance did any true apprehension become possible, a wordless trance of sheer feeling, an extra-physical state, in which nothing but the tingling of the finger-tips recalled the existence of the body, and a series of images floated across the mind, un-named, unrelated to language. That state, she supposed, was the state in which she approached most closely to the self concealed within her, but it was a state having nothing to do with Henry. Was this why she had welcomed, as the next best thing, the love which by its very pain gave her the illusion of contact?

She was, after all, a woman. Thwarted as an artist, was it perhaps possible to find fulfilment in other ways? Was there, after all, some foundation for the prevalent belief that woman should minister to man? Had the generations been right, the personal struggle wrong? Was there something beautiful, something active, something creative even, in her apparent submission to Henry? Could she not balance herself upon the tight-rope of her relationship with him, as dangerously and precariously as in the act of creating a picture? Was it not possible to see the tones and half-tones of her life with him as she might have seen the blue and violet shadows of a landscape; and so set them in relation and ordain their values, that she thereby forced them into beauty? Was not this also an achievement of the sort peculiarly suited to women? of the sort, indeed, which women alone could compass; a privilege, a prerogative, not to be despised? All the woman in her answered, yes! All the artist in her countered, no!

And then again, were not women in their new Protestant spirit defrauding the world of some poor remnant of enchantment, some illusion, foolish perhaps, but lovely? This time the woman and artist in her alike answered, yes.

She remembered a young couple she had known – the man a secretary at the Paris Embassy; very young they were – receiving her visits, as their ambassadress, with suitable reverence. She knew that they loved her, but at the same time she always felt her visits to be an intrusion. She divined them to be so much in love that they must grudge any half-hour filched from their allowance of years together. And she, for her part, counted her visits to them as an agony, yet she was drawn towards them partly from affection, partly from a desire to martyrise herself by the sight of their union. 'Male and female created he them,' she said to herself always, coming away. Sometimes, coming away, she felt herself to be so falsely placed in relation to Henry that the burden of life became too heavy, and she wished she might die. It was no phrase: she really wished it. She was too honest not to suffer under the burden of such falsity. She longed at times for a relationship as simple, as natural, and as right as the relationship between those two very uninteresting but engaging young people. She envied Alec as he stood before the fire jingling the coins in his pocket and looking down on his wife curled into a corner of the sofa. She envied Madge her unquestioning acceptance of everything that Alec said or did. Yet in the midst of her envy something offended her: this intolerably masculine lordliness, this abject feminine submission.

Where, then, lay the truth? Henry by the compulsion of love had cheated her of her chosen life, yet had given her another life, an ample life, a life in touch with the greater world, if that took her fancy; or a life, alternatively, pressed close up against her own nursery. For a life of her own, he had substituted his life with its interests, or the lives of her children with their potentialities. He assumed that she might sink herself in either, if not in both, with equal joy. It had never occurred to him that she might prefer simply to be herself.

A part of her had acquiesced. She remembered acquiescing in the assumption that she should project herself into the lives of her children, especially her sons, as though their entities were of far greater importance than her own, and she herself but the vehicle of their creation and the shelter of their vulnerable years. She remembered the birth of Kay. She had wanted to call him Kay, because just before his birth she had been reading Malory. Up till then, her sons had succeeded automatically to the family names – Herbert, Charles, Robert, William – but over the fifth son, for some reason, her wishes were consulted, and when she suggested Kay as a name Henry did not protest. He had been in a good humour and had said, 'Have it your own way.' She remembered that even in her weakness she had thought Henry generous. Looking down into the crumpled red face of her new baby – though crumpled red faces had become quite usual to her by then, at the sixth repetition – she had realised the responsibility of launching the little creature labelled by a name not of its own choosing, like launching a battleship, only instead of turrets and decks and guns she had to do with the miraculous tissue of flesh and brain. Was it fair to call a child Kay? A name, a label, exerted an unseen though continuous pressure. People were said to grow up in accordance with their names. But Kay, at any rate, had not grown up unduly romantic, though certainly he could not be said to resemble his brothers or elder sister.

Yet of all her children, Kay and Edith had alone inherited something of their mother – Kay with his astrolabes, Edith with her muddles. Carrie, characteristically, had given her least trouble; Carrie had managed her own way into the world. Herbert, as the eldest son, had arrived in pomp and with difficulty. William had been a mean, silent baby, with small eyes; greedy, too, as though determined to squeeze all the provision of her breast even as, to-day, he and Lavinia, his fitting mate, were determined to squeeze all their advantage from the local dairy. Charles had arrived protesting, even as he protested to-day, only at that time he knew nothing of War Offices. Edith had had to be beaten into drawing her first breath; she had been able to manage life no better at its beginning than at its end. The fact remained that in Kay and Edith alone she divined an unexpressed sympathy. All the rest were Henry's children, with his energy just gone wrong. Yet when her children were babies – small, prone things, or things so young and feeble that one could sit them up in safety only by supporting their insecure heads – she, trying to compensate herself for her foregone independence, had made an effort to look forward from the day when the skull over the pulse which so terrifyingly and openly throbbed should have closed up, when their hold on life would no longer be so alarmingly precarious, when she would no longer be afraid of their drawing their last breath even as she bent over their cradle in the absence of the nurse. She had tried to look forward to the day when they would develop characters of their own; when they would hold opinions different from their parents', when they would make plans and arrangements for themselves. Even in this, she had been suppressed, thwarted. 'How amused we shall be,' she had said to Henry as they stood together looking down on Herbert netted in his cot, 'when he starts writing us letters from school.' Henry had not liked that remark; she divined his criticism instantly. Henry thought that all real women ought to prefer their children helpless, and to deplore the day when they would begin to grow up. Long-clothes should be preferable to smocks; smocks to knickers; knickers to trousers. Henry had definite, masculine ideas about women and motherhood. Although secretly proud of his rising little sons, he pretended even to himself that they were, so far, entirely their mother's concern. So, naturally, she had endeavoured to adopt those views. Herbert, at two years old, had been deposed in favour of Carrie; Carrie, at a year, in favour of Charles. Because it was expected of her, the baby had always been officially her darling. But none of these things had held any truth in them. She had always been aware that the self of her children was as far removed from her as the self of Henry, or, indeed, her own.

Shocking, unnatural thoughts had floated into her mind. 'If only I had never married ... if only I had never had any children.'

Yet she loved Henry – to the point of agony – and she loved her children – to the point of sentimentality. She wove theories about them, which she confided to Henry in moments of privacy and expansion. Herbert would be a statesman, she said, for had he not questioned her (at the age of twelve) about problems of native government? And Kay, aged four, had asked to be taken to see the Taj Mahal. Henry had indulged her in these fancies, not seeing that she was, in fact, indulging him.

But all this had been as nothing compared with Henry's ambitions which drove her down a path hedged with thorns. Everything in Henry's conceptions of the world had run counter to her own grain. Realist and idealist, they represented the extreme opposites of their points of view, with the difference that whereas Henry need make no bones about his creed, she must protect hers from shame and ridicule. Yet there, again, confusion swathed her. There were moments when she could enter into the excitement of the great game that Henry was always playing; moments when the private, specialised, intense, and lovely existence of the artist – whose practice had been denied her, but after whose ideal of life she still miserably and imaginatively hankered – seemed a poor and selfish and over-delicate thing compared with the masculine business of empire and politics and the strife of men. There were moments when she could understand not only with her brain but with her sensibility, that Henry should crave for a life of action even as she herself craved for a life of contemplation. They were indeed two halves of one dissevered world.

PART THREE

This Life we live is dead for all its breath;
Death's self it is, set off on pilgrimage,
Travelling with tottering steps the first short stage.

CHRISTINA ROSSETTI

soigner. Elle ferait beaucoup mieux, beaucoup, se vieille Genoux. Les premiers jours il faisait chaud, c'est vrai; ce qu'il y a de plus malin, c'est que avec le soleil sans crier gare, à l'âge de malade se ne doit pas prendre de libertés. Don't hurry me till you mood. Genoux,' said Lady Slane, as going from her early bath and precautions alike.

Summer over, the October days were no longer warm enough for Lady Slane to sit in the garden. In order to get her airing she must go for a little walk, loaded with cloaks and furs by Genoux, who accompanied her to the front door to make sure that she did not discard any of her wrappings in the hall on the way. Lady Slane sometimes protested, as Genoux dragged one garment after another from the cupboard. 'But, Genoux, you are making me look like an old bundle.' Genoux, hanging the last cloak firmly round her shoulders, replied, 'Miladi est bien trop distinguée pour avoir jamais l'air d'un vieux bundle.' 'Do you remember, Genoux,' said Lady Slane, drawing on her gloves, 'how you always wanted me to wear woollen stockings for dinner?' It was indeed true. Genoux in cold weather had never been willing to put out silk stockings with her mistress's evening dress; or if she put them, after many remonstrances, she hopefully put also a woollen pair to wear underneath. 'Mais pourquoi pas, miladi?' said Genoux sensibly; 'dans ce temps-là les dames, même les jeunes dames, portaient les jupes conven-ablement longues, et un jupon par dessus le marché. Pourquoi s'enrhumer, pour des chevilles qui n'y paraissent pas? C'était la même histoire pour les combinaisons que miladi voulait à tout prix ôter pour le dîner, précisément au soir lorsqu'il fait plus froid.' She accompanied Lady Slane downstairs, talking in this strain, for all her volubility had been released since quitting Elm Park Gardens and the household of English servants with their cold discreet ways. She hovered and clucked over Lady Slane, half-scolding, half-cherishing. 'Miladi n'a jamais su se soigner. Elle ferait beaucoup mieux d'écouter sa vieille Genoux. Les premiers jours d'octobre, c'est tout ce qu'il y a de plus malin. Ça vous attrape sans crier gare. A l'âge de miladi on ne doit pas prendre de libertés.' 'Don't bury me till you need, Genoux,' said Lady Slane, escaping from her Anglicisms and pessimism alike.

She went down the steps carefully, for there had been a frost and they might be slippery. Genoux would watch her out of sight, she knew, so at the corner she must turn round to wave. Genoux would be hurt if she forgot to turn round. Yet by the gesture she would not be reassured; she would not be happy again until she had readmitted the muffled figure of the old lady to the safety of the house; drawn her in, taken off her boots, brought her slippers and perhaps a cup of hot soup, carried away her wraps, and left her to her book beside the sitting-room fire. Yet Genoux, for all her adages and croakings, was a gay and philosophical old soul, full of wisdom of the sturdy peasant kind. (She waved back to Lady Slane as Lady Slane after dutifully looking round turned the corner and pursued her way slowly towards the Heath.) Now she would go back to the kitchen and talk to the cat while she busied herself with her pots and pans. Lady Slane frequently heard her talking to the cat, 'Viens, mon bo-bo,' she would say; 'nice dinner, look, that's all for you,' – for she had an idea that English animals understood English only, and once, hearing the jackals bark round Gul-a-hek, had remarked to Lady Slane, 'C'est drôle tout de même, miladi, comme on entend tout de suite que ce ne sont pas des Anglais.' Well, it was a gentle life they led now, she and Genoux, thought Lady Slane making her way slowly up the hill towards the Heath; she and Genoux, living in such undisturbed intimacy, bound by the ties respectively of gratitude and devotion, bound also by the tie of their unspoken speculation as to which would be taken from the other first. Whenever the front door shut behind one of their rare visitors, each was conscious of a certain relief at the departure of intruders. The routine of their daily life was all they wanted – all, indeed, that they had strength for. Effort tired them both, though they had never admitted it to one another.

Fortunately, the intruders came but seldom. Lady Slane's children had come first, in rotation, as a duty, but most of them indicated to their mother so clearly the extreme inconvenience of coming as far as Hampstead that she felt justified in begging them to spare themselves the trouble, and except at intervals they took her at her word. Lady Slane was quite shrewd enough to imagine what they said to one another to appease their consciences: 'Well, we *asked* Mother to make her home with us ...' Edith alone had shown some disposition to come frequently and, as she called it, help. But Edith was now living in such a state of bliss in her own flat, that she had been easily able to decide that her mother didn't really want her. Kay she had not seen for some time. Last time he came, he had said after a great deal of shuffling and embarrassment that a friend of his, old FitzGeorge, wanted to be brought to call upon her. 'I think,' said Kay, poking the fire, 'that he said he had met you in India.' 'In India?' said Lady Slane vaguely. 'It's quite possible, dear, but I don't remember the name. So many people came, you see. We were often twenty to luncheon. Could you put him off, do you think, Kay? I don't want to be rude, but somehow I seem to have lost my taste for strangers.'

Kay longed to ask his mother what Fitz had meant by saying he had seen him in his cradle. He had in fact come up to Hampstead determined to clear up this mystery. But, of course, he went away without asking.

No great-grandchildren. They were forbidden. The grandchildren did not count; they were insignificant as the middle distance. But the great-grandchildren, who were not insignifi-cant, but might be disturbing, were forbidden. Lady Slane had adhered to that, with the strange firmness sometimes and sud-denly displayed by the most docile people. Mr Bucktrout was the only regular visitor, coming once a week to tea, on Tuesdays. But she was not tired by Mr Bucktrout; they would sit on either side of the fire, not lighting the lamps, while Mr Bucktrout's conversation ran on like a purling brook, and Lady Slane listened or not, as she felt inclined.

Meanwhile, it was very beautiful, up on the Heath, with the brown trees and the blue distance. Lady Slane sat down on a bench and rested. Little boys were flying kites; they ran drag-ging the string across the turf, till like an ungainly bird the kite rose trailing its untidy tail across the sky. Lady Slane remem-bered other little boys flying kites in China. Her foreign memories and her English present played at *chassé-croisé* often now in her mind, mingling and superimposing, making her wonder sometimes whether her memory were not becoming a little confused, so immediate and simultaneous did both impres-sions appear. Was she on a hillside near Pekin with Henry, a groom walking their horses up and down at a respectful dis-tance; or was she alone, old, and dressed in black, resting on a bench on Hampstead Heath? But there were the chimney-pots of London to steady her. No doubt about it, these little boys were Cockneys in rags, not celestial urchins in blue cotton; and her own limbs, as she shifted her position a little on the hard bench, gave her a rheumatic tweak bearing no relation to her young and physical well-being as she cantered up the scorched hillside with Henry. She tried, in a dim and groping way, to revive the sensation of that well-being. She found it impossi-ble. A dutiful inner voice summoned from the past as some old melody might float unseizable into the outskirts of recol-lection, reproduced for her in words the facts of that sensation without awakening any response in her dulled old body. In vain she now told herself that once she had woken up on a summer morning longing to spring from her bed and to run out for sheer exuberance of spirit into the air. In vain she tried, and most deliberately, to renew the sharpness of waiting for the moment when – their official life suspended – she would turn in the darkness into Henry's arms. It was all words now, without reality. The only things which touched reality were the routine of her life with Genoux; the tiny interests of that life – the tradesmen's ring at the back door, the arrival of a parcel of books from Mudie's, the consultation as to Mr Bucktrout's Tuesday tea, should they buy muffins or crumpets? the agitation over an announced visit from Carrie; and then the growth of her bodily ailments, for which she was beginning to feel quite an affection. Her body had, in fact, become her companion, a constant resource and preoccupation; all the small squalors of the body, known only to oneself, insignificant in youth, easily dismissed, in old age became dominant and entered into fulfilment of the tyranny they had always threatened. Yet it was, rather than otherwise, an agreeable and interesting tyranny. A hint of lumbago caused her to rise cautiously from her chair and reminded her of the day she had ricked her back at Nervi, since when her back had never been very reliable. The small intimacies of her teeth were known to her, so that she ate carefully, biting on one side rather than on the other. She instinctively crooked one finger – the third on the left hand – to save it from the pang of neuritis. An in-growing toe-nail obliged Genoux to use the shoe-horn with the greatest precaution. And all these parts of the body became intensely personal: my back, my tooth, my finger, my toe; and Genoux, again, was the only person who knew exactly what she meant by a sudden exclamation as she fell back into her chair, the bond between herself and Genoux thereby strengthening to the pitch of the bond between lovers, of an exclusive physical intimacy. Of such small things was her life now made: of communion with Genoux, of interest in her own disintegrating body, of Mr Bucktrout's courtesy and weekly visits, of her pleasure in the frosty morning and the little boys flying kites on the Heath; even of her anxiety about slipping upon a frozen doorstep, for the bones of the aged, she knew, were brittle. All tiny things, contemptibly tiny things, ennobled only by their vast background, the background of Death. Certain Italian paintings depicted trees – poplar, willow, alder – each leaf separate, and sharp, and veined, against a green translucent sky. Of such a quality were the tiny things, the shapely leaves, of her present life: redeemed from insignificance by their juxtaposition with a luminous eternity.

She felt exalted, she escaped from an obvious pettiness, from a finicking life, whenever she remembered that no adventure could now befall her except the supreme adventure for which all other adventures were but a preparation.

She miscalculated, however, forgetting that life's surprises were inexhaustible, even up to the end. On re-entering her house that afternoon she found a man's hat of peculiar square shape reposing upon the hall table, and Genoux in a state of excitement greeted her with a whisper: 'Miladi! il y a un monsieur ... je lui ai dit que miladi était sortie, mais c'est un monsieur qui n'écoute pas ... il attend miladi au salon. Faut-il servir le thé? – Miladi ôtera bien ses souliers, de peur qu'ils ne soient humides?'

Lady Slane looked back upon her meeting with Mr FitzGeorge. So did Mr FitzGeorge look back upon his meeting with Lady Slane. Having waited long enough, and vainly, for Kay to bring him, he had taken the law into his own hands and had come by himself. Miserly in spite of his millions, he had travelled up to Hampstead by Underground; had walked from the station; had paused before Lady Slane's house, and with the eye of a connoisseur had appreciated its Georgian dignity. 'Ah,' he had said with satisfaction, 'the house of a woman of taste.' He soon discovered his error, for, having over-ridden Genoux's objections and pushed his way into the hall, he found that Lady Slane had no taste at all. Perversely, this delighted him the more. The room into which Genoux reluctantly showed him was simple and comfortable. 'Arm-chairs and chintz, and the light in the right place,' he muttered, wandering about. He was extraordinarily moved at the prospect of seeing Lady Slane again. But when she came it was obvious that she did not remember him in the least. She greeted him politely, with a return to the viceregal manner; apologised for her absence, asked him to sit down; said that Kay had mentioned his name; said that tea would come in a minute; but was manifestly puzzled as to what errand had brought him. Perhaps she wondered whether he wished to write her husband's life? Mr FitzGeorge, as this reflection struck him, cackled suddenly, and, to his hostess, inexplicably. He could scarcely explain at once that the Vicereine and not the Viceroy had touched his imagination, more than half a century ago, at Calcutta.

As it was, he was compelled to explain that, as a young man, he had come with letters of introduction to Government House and had perfunctorily been asked to dinner. Mr FitzGeorge, however, was not embarrassed; he was too genuinely detached from such social conventions. He accounted for himself quite simply and without evasions. 'You see,' he said, 'I was a nameless young man, to whom an unknown father had left a large fortune, with the wish that I should travel round the world. I was naturally delighted to avail myself of such an opportunity. It is always pleasant to gratify wishes which coincide with one's own. The solicitors, who were also my guardians,' he added dryly, 'commended my promptitude in complying with the wish expressed in the will. In their view, old dotards mouldering in Lincoln's Inn, a young man who would desert London for the far East at his father's suggestion was a filial young man indeed. I suppose they thought the stage-doors of Shaftesbury Avenue a greater attraction than the bazaars of Canton. Well, they erred. Half the treasures of my collection to-day, Lady Slane, I owe to that journey round the world sixty years ago.'

It was clear that Lady Slane had never heard of his collection. She said as much. He was delighted, much as he had been delighted when he discovered that she had no taste.

'Capital, Lady Slane! My collection is, I suppose, at least twice as valuable as that of Eumorphopoulos, and twice as famous – though, I may add, I have paid a hundredth part of its present value for it. And, unlike most experts, I have never lost sight of beauty. Rarity, curiosity, antiquity are not enough for me. I must have beauty or, at any rate, craftmanship. And I have been justified. There is no piece in my collection to-day which any museum would not despoil its best show-case to possess.'

Lady Slane, knowing nothing of such things, was amused by such innocently childish boastfulness. She egged him on, this naïf old magpie, this collector of beautiful objects, who had suddenly made his way into her house, and now sat by her fire, bragging, forgetting that dinner-party at Calcutta and his friendship with Kay, which alone could have justified his intrusion. He had for her, from the first moment, the charm of a completely detached and isolated figure. The very fact that he had no known parents and no legitimate name, but was purely and simply himself, invested him with a certain legendary charm in her eyes. She had had enough, in her life, of people whose worldly status was their passport to admission. Mr FitzGeorge had no such passport; even his wealth could scarcely be considered a passport, for his reputation as a miser instantly destroyed the hopes of the most sanguine seeker after benefit. Curiously enough, Lady Slane was not offended by his avarice as she was offended by it in her own son William. William and Lavinia were furtively avaricious; they couldn't help being stingy, since parsimony ran in their blood – she remembered thinking when they became engaged that that was the real link between them – but they were not frank about it, they tried to cover it up. Mr FitzGeorge indulged his weakness on the grander scale, making no bones about it. Lady Slane liked people who, if they had vices, were not ashamed of them. She despised all hypocritical disguises. So when Mr FitzGeorge told her that he hated parting with money, could only be induced to do so when irresistibly tempted by beauty, and could console himself only by the lure of a bargain, she frankly laughed and frankly gave him her respect. He looked at her across the fire. His coat, she observed, was shabby. 'I remember,' he said, 'that you laughed at me in Calcutta.'

He seemed to remember a great many things about Calcutta. 'Lady Slane,' he said, fencing, when she taxed him with his excellent memory, 'have you not yet noticed that youthful memories sharpen with advancing age?' That little 'yet' made her laugh again: he was playing the part of a man pretending to a woman that she still retained her youth. She was eighty-eight, but the man-to-woman mainspring still coiled like a cobra between them. Innumerable years had elapsed since she had felt that stimulus; it came as an unexpected revival, a flicker, a farewell, stirring her strangely and awaking some echo whose melody she could not quite recapture. Had she really seen FitzGeorge before, or did his slight and old-fashioned gallantry awaken only the general memory of years when all men had looked at her with admiration in their eyes? Whichever it was, his presence disquieted her, though she could not pretend that her faint agitation was anything but pleasant, and he had looked at her, too, in such a way as to suggest that he could provide her with the explanation if he would. All the evening, after he had gone, she sat gazing into the fire, her book neglected, wondering, trying to remember, trying to put her hand on something that remained tantalisingly just round the corner, just out of reach. Something had knocked against her as the clapper might knock against a cracked old bell in a disused steeple. No music travelled out over the valleys, but within the steeple itself a tingling vibration arose, disturbing the starlings in their nests and causing the cobwebs to quiver.

Next morning she, of course, derided her evening mood. What queer freak of sentimentality had caught her? For two hours she had been as dreamy as a girl! It was FitzGeorge's fault for entering her house in that way, for sitting down beside her fire as though he had some right to be there, for talking about the past, for teasing her gently about her dignity as the young Vicereine, for looking at her as though he were saying only half of what he would say later on, for being slightly mocking, slightly gallant, wholly admiring, and, secretly, moved. Although he had preserved a surface manner, she knew that his visit had not been without import to him. She wondered whether he would come again.

If the gentleman returned, said Genoux, was he to be admitted? Next time she would be prepared for him; he should not brush her aside as though she were yesterday's newspaper and walk straight into the hall, laying his funny little hat on the table. 'Ah, mon Dieu, miladi, quel drôle de chapeau!' She doubled herself up, rubbing her hands down her thighs as she laughed. Lady Slane loved Genoux's whole-hearted enjoyment of anything that struck her as funny. In response, she permitted herself a smile at Mr FitzGeorge's hat. Where did he get such hats? asked Genoux; car jamais je n'ai vu un pareil chapeau en devanture. Did he have them made purposely for himself alone? And his muffler – had her ladyship seen it? All checks, like a stud-groom. 'C'est un original,' Genoux concluded sagely; but, unlike an English servant, she was not interested merely in making fun of Mr FitzGeorge. She wanted to know more about him. It was pathetic, she said, to be like that – un vieux monsieur, and all alone. Had he never been married? He did not look as though he had been married. She followed Lady Slane about, eager for the information Lady Slane was unable to provide. He had made a good tea, said Genoux; she had noticed the shabbiness of his coat, assuming an excessive poverty: 'J'ai vite couru au coin de la rue, attraper l'homme aux muffins;' and was noticeably disappointed when Lady Slane told her rather dryly that Mr FitzGeorge, to the best of her knowledge, was a millionaire. 'Un milliardaire! et s'affubler comme ça!' Genoux could not get over it. But what was the long and short of it to be? she asked. Was she to let him in next time, or was she not?

Lady Slane said she did not suppose Mr FitzGeorge would come again, but even as she said it she detected herself in a lie, for as he took his leave, Mr FitzGeorge had kept her hand and had asked for permission to return. Why should she lie to Genoux? 'Yes, let him in,' she said, moving away towards her sitting-room.

There were three of them now, three old gentlemen – Mr Bucktrout, Mr Gosheron, and Mr FitzGeorge. A funny trio – an agent, a builder, and a connoisseur! all old, all eccentric, and all unworldly. How oddly it had come about, that the whole of her life should have fallen away from her – her activities, her children, and Henry – and should have been so completely replaced in this little interlude before the end by a new existence so satisfyingly populated! She supposed that she herself was responsible for its creation, but could not imagine how she had done it. 'Perhaps,' she said aloud, 'one always gets what one wants in the end.' And taking down an old book, she opened it at random and read:

> Cease of your oaths, cease of your great swearing,
> Cease of your pomp, cease of your vainglory,
> Cease of your hate, cease of your blaspheming,
> Cease of your malice, cease of your envy,
> Cease of your wrath, cease of your lechery,
> Cease of your fraud, cease your deception,
> Cease of your tongues making detraction.

It was surely remarkable that someone should have expressed her longing in – she looked at the date – 1493?

She read the next verse:

> Flee faint falsehood, fickle, foul, and fell,
> Flee fatal flatterers, full of fairness,
> Flee fair feigning, fables of favell,
> Flee folks' fellowship, frequenting falseness,
> Flee frantic facers fulfilled of frowardness,
> Flee fools' fallacies, flee fond fantasies,
> Flee from fresh babblers, feigning flatteries.

She had fled them all, except the fond fantasies; her three old gentlemen were fond fantasies – fond fantasticks, she amended, smiling. As for pomp, vainglory, and tongues making detraction, they were things that never crossed her threshold now except when Carrie brought them in on a gust of chilly air. Then she caught herself up for so readily adopting Mr FitzGeorge and adding him to her intimates: what reason had she to suppose, beyond a phrase spoken in parting civility, that he would ever come again?

He came again, and she heard Genoux welcoming him as an old friend in the hall. Yes, her ladyship was in; yes, her ladyship had said she would be delighted to receive monsieur at any time. Lady Slane listened, wishing that Genoux would not be quite so hospitable on her behalf. She was not at all sure, now, that she liked her privacy being laid open to invasion by Mr FitzGeorge. She must ask Kay to drop him a hint.

Meanwhile she received him, rising in her soft black draperies and giving him her hand with the smile he remembered. Why should she not? After all, they were two old people, very old people, so old that they were all the time age-conscious, and being so old it was agreeable to sit like two cats on either side of the fire warming their bones, stretching out hands so transparent as to let the pink light of the flames through them, while their conversation without effort rose or fell. Lady Slane, all her life long, had made people feel that they could talk if they liked, but need not talk if disinclined – one of the reasons why Henry Holland had first decided to marry her. Having a fund of quietness within herself, she could understand that other people also enjoyed being quiet. Few women, Henry Holland said, could be quiet without being dull, and fewer women could talk without being a bore; but then Henry Holland, although he enjoyed women, had a low opinion of them and was satisfied by none except his own wife. FitzGeorge with really remarkable shrewdness had diagnosed this in Calcutta where the Viceroy, heaven knows, had been sufficiently surrounded by pretty and animated women all flatteringly deluded by the apparently close and exclusive attention he accorded to each one in turn.

Thank goodness, thought Mr FitzGeorge, she has no taste. He was sick to death of women who prided themselves on their taste, and thereby assumed an understanding with him as a connoisseur. There was no relation between the two things, –

between 'decoration' and real beauty. His works of art belonged to a different world from the skilful interiors of women of taste. He looked almost tenderly at Lady Slane's pink shaded lamps and Turkey rug. If one wanted beauty, one had only to rest one's eyes on her, so fine and old and lovely, like an ivory carving; flowing down like water into her chair, so slight and supple were her limbs, the firelight casting a flush of rose over her features and snowy hair. Youth had no beauty like the beauty of an old face; the face of youth was an unwritten page. Youth could never sit as still as that, in absolute repose, as though all haste, all movement, were over and done with, and nothing left but waiting and acquiescence. He was glad that he had never seen her in the middle years, so that he might keep untarnished his memory of her when she was young, lively, and full of fire, completing it with this present vision of her, having arrived at the other end of the story. The same woman, but he himself in ignorance of what had happened in between.

He became aware that he had not spoken for quite five minutes. Lady Slane appeared to have forgotten him. Yet she was not asleep, for she was looking quietly into the fire, her hands lying loose in their usual attitude, and her foot resting on the fender. He was surprised that she should accept him so naturally. 'But we are old,' he thought, 'and our perceptions are muted. She takes it for granted that I should sit here as though I had known her all my life. Lady Slane,' he said aloud, 'I don't believe you took much pleasure in your viceroyalty?'

His voice was always rather harsh and sardonic, and even in her company he made no attempt to soften it. He disregarded and despised mankind so much that he seldom spoke without a sneer. Kay was his only friend, but even Kay got the rough side of his tongue oftener than the smooth.

Lady Slane stiffened, out of a reviving loyalty to Henry. 'Even viceroyalty has its uses, Mr FitzGeorge.'

'But not for such as you,' Mr FitzGeorge said, unrepentant. 'Do you know,' he said, leaning forward, 'I was really upset by seeing you trapped among those mummers. You submitted and did your part – oh, admirably! – but all the time you were denying your nature. I remember waiting for you and Lord Slane to appear before dinner; we were assembled in some big drawing-room, thirty of us, I daresay, people wearing jewels and uniforms, all standing about feeling more or less foolish on an immense expanse of carpet. I remember there was a huge chandelier all lit up with candles; it tinkled whenever anybody walked overhead. I wondered whether it was your footstep that made it tinkle. And then a great folding-door was thrown open and you came in with the Viceroy, and all the women curtsied. After dinner you both came round the circle of your guests, saying something to each; you wore white, with diamonds in your hair, and you asked me if I hoped to get any big-game shooting. I suppose you thought that was the right thing to say to a rich young man; you couldn't know that I abominated the idea of killing animals. I said no, I was just a traveller; but although you smiled attentively I don't believe you listened to my answer. You were thinking what you should say to the next person, and no doubt you said something just as well composed and just as inappropriate. It was the Viceroy, not you, who suggested that I should accompany you on your trip.'

'On our trip?' said Lady Slane, amazed.

'You know that easy amiable way he had of throwing out suggestions? Half the time one knew that he didn't mean what he said, and that he never expected one to act upon it. One was expected to bow and say, Thank you so much, that would be delightful, and then never to refer to it again. He would say, China? yes, I am going to China next week; very interesting country, China; you ought to come with me. But he would have been very much surprised if one had taken him at his word, though I daresay that with his perfect manners he would have concealed his surprise. Now, Lady Slane, isn't it true?'

Without waiting to hear whether it were true, he went on. 'But on this one occasion somebody did take him at his word. I did. He said, You're an antiquarian, FitzGeorge – antiquarian for him was a vague term – you're an antiquarian, he said, and you're in no hurry. Why don't you come with us to Fatihpur Sikhri?'

The broken puzzle in Lady Slane's mind shook itself suddenly down into shape. The half-heard notes reassembled themselves into their tune. She stood again on the terrace of the deserted Indian city looking across the brown landscape where puffs of rising dust marked at intervals the road to Agra. She leant her arms upon the warm parapet and slowly twirled her parasol. She twirled it because she was slightly ill at ease. She and the young man beside her were isolated from the rest of the world. The Viceroy was away from them, inspecting the mother-of-pearl mosque, accompanied by a group of officials in white uniforms and sun-helmets; he was pointing with his stick, and saying that the ring-doves ought to be cleared away from under the eaves. The young man beside Lady Slane said softly that it was a pity the ring-doves should be condemned, for if a city were abandoned by man, why should the doves not inherit it? The doves, the monkeys, and the parrots, he went on, as a flight of jade-green parakeets swept past them, quarrelling in the air; look at their green plumage against these damask walls, he added, raising his head, as the flock swirled round again like a handful of emeralds blown across the Poet's House. There was something unusual, he said, in a city of mosques, palaces, and courts, inhabited solely by birds and animals; he would like to see a tiger going up Akbar's steps, and a cobra coiling its length neatly in the council chamber. They would be more becoming, he thought, to the red city than men in boots and solar topees. Lady Slane, keeping an ear pricked to observe the movements of the Viceroy and his group, had smiled at his fancies and had said that Mr FitzGeorge was a romantic.

Mr FitzGeorge. The name came back to her now. It was not surprising that, among so many thousands of names, she should have forgotten it. But she remembered it now, as she remembered the look he had given her when she twitted him. It was more than a look; it was a moment that he created, while he held her eyes and filled them with all the implications he dared not, or would not, speak. She had felt as though she stood naked before him.

'Yes,' he said, watching her across the fire at Hampstead; 'you were right: I *was* a romantic.'

She was startled to hear him thus audibly joining up with her recollections; the moment, then, had possessed equal significance, equal intensity, for him as for her? Its significance had indeed troubled her, and, for a while, made her more uneasy than she would acknowledge. Her loyalty to Henry was impeccable; but after the departure of FitzGeorge, that stray young traveller whose name her consciousness had scarcely registered, she had felt as though someone had exploded a charge of dynamite in her most secret cellar. Someone by a look had discovered the way into a chamber she kept hidden even from herself. He had committed the supreme audacity of looking into her soul.

'It was queer, wasn't it?' he said, still watching her.

'And after you left us at Agra,' said Lady Slane conversationally, unwilling to admit that he had shaken her, 'what did you do?'

'I went up into Cashmir,' said Mr FitzGeorge, leaning back in his chair and putting his fingertips together; 'I went up the river for a fortnight in a houseboat. I had plenty of time to think, and while I gazed over lakes of pink lotus I thought of a young woman in a white dress, so dutiful, so admirably trained, and so wild at heart. I used to flatter myself that for a minute I had come close to her, and then I remembered how after one glance she had turned away and had sauntered off towards her husband. But whether she did it because she was frightened, or because she intended to rebuke me, I could never decide. Perhaps both.'

'If she was frightened,' said Lady Slane, surprising both herself and FitzGeorge, 'it was of herself, not of you.'

'I didn't flatter myself it was of me,' said Mr FitzGeorge; 'I knew even then that I had no charm for women, especially for lovely, eminent young women like yourself. I didn't desire it,' he said, looking at her as defiantly as his rather absurd old-maidish appearance would allow.

'Of course you didn't,' said Lady Slane, respecting this flicker of a thwarted pride.

'No,' said Mr FitzGeorge, relapsing appeased; 'I didn't. And yet, you know,' he added, stung by some recollection to a fresh honesty, 'although I had never fallen in love with a woman before, and never have since, I fell in love with you at Fatihpur Sikhri. I suppose I really fell in love with you at that ridiculous dinner-party at Calcutta. Otherwise I should not have come to Fatihpur Sikhri. It took me out of my way, and I have never gone out of my way for man, woman, or child. I am the complete egoist, Lady Slane; you had better know it. Nothing but a work of art could tempt me out of my way. In China, where I went after Cashmir, I was so intoxicated by the works of art that I soon forgot you.'

This strange, incivil, and retarded love-making created a medley of feelings in Lady Slane. It offended her loyalty to Henry. It disturbed her old-age peacefulness. It revived the perplexities of her youth. It shocked her slightly, and pleased her more than it shocked. It was the very last thing she had ever expected – she whose days were now made up of retrospect and of only one anticipation. It was as though Mr FitzGeorge had arrived with deliberate and malicious purpose to do violence to her settled mood.

'But even in China,' Mr FitzGeorge went on, 'I still found leisure to think of you and Lord Slane. You seemed to me ill-assorted, as one might say of biscuits, only with biscuits one always assumes that it is the other way round. By saying that you were ill-assorted I don't mean to imply that you did not do your job admirably. You did. So admirably, that it awoke my suspicions. What would you have done with your life, Lady Slane, had you not married that very delightful and discon-certing charlatan?'

'Charlatan, Mr FitzGeorge?'

'Oh no, of course he wasn't altogether a charlatan,' said Mr FitzGeorge; 'on the contrary, he managed to be an undisastrous Prime Minister of England during five (I am told) difficult years. Nearly all years, incidentally, are difficult. Perhaps I misjudge him. But you will admit that he was handicapped. He had more charm than any man I ever knew; and though charm pays up to a certain point, there comes a point beyond which no reasonable man can be expected to go. He went beyond it – far beyond. He was too good to be true. You your-self, Lady Slane, must often have suffered from his charm?'

The question was proffered in such a way that Lady Slane nearly replied to it truthfully and inadvertently. Mr FitzGeorge seemed really interested; and yet, she remem-bered, she had often watched Henry bending his brows in interest over some human question which could not really interest him at all, withdrawn as he was into a world where human interests shrank to insignificance, and nothing but a cold, sardonic ambition lay at the kernel of his mind, and if so

Henry, then why not Mr FitzGeorge? The one was a statesman, the other a connoisseur; she did not want to be examined as though she were a Tang figure which might possibly turn out to be a fake. Observation of Henry had taught her a lesson she would not easily forget. It had been terrible to live with, and to love, a being so charming, so deceptive, and so chill. Henry, she discovered suddenly, had been a very masculine man; masculinity, in spite of his charm and his culture, was the keynote of his character. He was of the world worldly, for all his scorn.

'I should have been a painter,' said Lady Slane, answering the question before last.

'Ah!' said Mr FitzGeorge with the relief of a man who has at last secured what he wanted. 'Thank you. That gives me the key. So you were an artist, were you, potentially? But being a woman, that had to go by the board. I see. Now I understand why you sometimes looked so tragic when your face was in repose. I remember looking at you and thinking, That is a woman whose heart is broken.'

'My dear Mr FitzGeorge!' cried Lady Slane. 'You really mustn't talk as though my life had been a tragedy. I had everything that most women would covet: position, comfort, children, and a husband I loved. I had nothing to complain of – nothing.'

'Except that you were defrauded of the one thing that mattered. Nothing matters to an artist except the fulfilment of his gift. You know that as well as I do. Frustrated, he grows crooked like a tree twisted into an unnatural shape. All meaning goes out of life, and life becomes existence – a makeshift. Face it, Lady Slane. Your children, your husband, your splendour, were nothing but obstacles that kept you from yourself. They were what you chose to substitute for your real vocation. You were too young, I suppose, to know any better, but when you chose that life you sinned against the light.'

Lady Slane put her hand over her eyes. She was no longer strong enough to bear this shock of denouncement. Mr FitzGeorge, suddenly inspired like a preacher, had overturned her placidity without any pity.

'Yes,' she said weakly, 'I know you are right.'

'Of course I am right. Old Fitz may be a comic figure, but he retains some sense of values, and I see that you have offended against one of the first canons of my creed. No wonder that I scold.'

'Don't scold me any more,' said Lady Slane, looking up and smiling; 'I assure you that if I did wrong, I paid for it. But you mustn't blame my husband.'

'I don't. According to his lights, he gave you all you could desire. He merely killed you, that's all. Men do kill women. Most women enjoy being killed; so I am told. Being a woman, I daresay that even you took a certain pleasure in the process. And now, are you angry with me?'

'No,' said Lady Slane; 'I think it is rather a relief to have been found out.'

'Of course you realise that I found you out at Fatihpur Sikhri? Not in detail, certainly, but in principle. This conversation is only a sequel to the conversation we didn't have then.'

Shaken though she was, Lady Slane laughed frankly. She felt immensely grateful to the outrageous Mr FitzGeorge, who, now that he had ceased to scold her, sat looking at her with humour and affection.

'A conversation interrupted for fifty years,' she said.

'And now never to be resumed,' he said with surprising tact, knowing that she might dread a repeated probing of his lancet into her discovered wound; 'but there are some things which need to be said – this was one of them. Now we can be friends.'

Having thus arranged their friendship, Mr FitzGeorge took it quite for granted that she should welcome his company. He arrived without warning, installed himself in what rapidly became his own chair, teased Genoux who adored him, carried on extravagant discussions with Mr Bucktrout, imposed his habits on the house, but nevertheless fitted himself neatly in to Lady Slane's ways of life. He even accompanied her on her slow and shaky walks up to the Heath. Her capes, and his square hat, became familiar objects moving under the wintry trees. They wandered tremulously together, often sitting down on a bench, not admitting to one another that they were tired, but pretending that they desired to admire the view. When they had admired it long enough to feel rested, they agreed to get up and go a little farther. Thus they revived memories of Constable, and even visited Keats' house, that little white box of strain and tragedy marooned among the dark green laurels. Like ghosts themselves, they murmured of the ghost of Fanny Brawne and of the passion which had wrecked Keats; and all the while, just out of reach, round the corner, lurked the passion for Lady Slane which might have wrecked Mr FitzGeorge, had he not been so wary an egoist (unlike poor Keats), just too wise to let himself float away on a hopeless love for the young Vicereine, just unwise enough to remain remotely faithful for fifty years.

Up on the Heath one day he recalled her to an incident she had forgotten.

'Do you remember,' he said – those three opening words having become so familiar to them that now they smiled whenever they used them – 'that the day after that dinner-party I came back to luncheon?'

'Dinner-party?' said Lady Slane vaguely, for her mind no longer worked very quickly. 'What dinner-party?'

'At Calcutta,' he said gently, for he never grew impatient when she had to be prompted. 'The Viceroy asked me back to luncheon when I had accepted to meet you at Fatihpur Sikhri. He said we must arrange the details. I arrived rather early, and found you alone. Not quite alone, though. Kay was with you.'

'Kay?' said Lady Slane. 'Oh, but surely Kay wasn't born then.'

'He was two months old. You had him in the room with you, in his crib. Don't you remember? You were rather embarrassed at being found with your baby by a strange young man. But you got over your embarrassment at once – I remember admiring the simplicity of your manners – and asked me to look at him. You held back the curtain of his crib, and for your sake I did give one glance at the horrid little object, but what I really looked at was your hand holding back the curtain. It was as white as the muslin, and stained only with the colour of your rings.'

'These rings,' said Lady Slane, touching the bumps under her black gloves.

'If you say so. I once told Kay I had seen him in his cradle,' said Mr FitzGeorge, chuckling. 'I had been saving up that joke against him for years. I startled him, I can tell you. But I gave him no explanation. To this day he doesn't know. Unless he asked you?'

'No,' said Lady Slane, 'he never asked me. And if he had asked me I shouldn't have been able to tell him.'

'No; one forgets, one forgets,' said Mr FitzGeorge, staring out over the Heath. 'Yet there are some things one never forgets. I remember your hand on the curtain, and I remember your expression as you looked down on that nasty little new thing which has grown up into Kay. I remember the twisted

131

feeling it gave me, to have stumbled into your intimacy. It didn't last long. You rang the bell, and a nurse came and removed Kay complete with his furniture.'

'Are you fond of Kay?' asked Lady Slane.

'Fond?' said Mr FitzGeorge, astonished. 'Well – I'm used to him. Yes, I suppose you might say I was fond. We understand each other well enough to let each other alone. We're used to each other – put it like that. At our age, anything else would be a nuisance.'

Fondness, indeed, seemed a remote thing even to Lady Slane. She was fond of Mr FitzGeorge, she supposed, and of Genoux, and of Mr Bucktrout, and in a less degree of Mr Gosheron, but it was a fondness out of which all the trouble and the agitation had departed. Even as the vitality had departed out of her old body. All emotion now was a twilight thing. She could say no more than that it was pleasant to stroll and sit on the Heath with Mr FitzGeorge while he evoked memories of a day whose light, even through those veils, flared up too strongly for her faded eyes.

Even so, Mr FitzGeorge had not told Lady Slane the whole of the truth. He had not reminded her that when he came that day and found her alone with Kay in his cradle in a corner of the room, he had also found her kneeling on the floor surrounded by a mass of flowers. To his idea, fresh from England, the season was winter; yet, cut from an Indian garden, roses, larkspurs, and sweet-peas lay sorted into heaps around her. Transparent glasses filled with water made points of light as they stood about all over the carpet. She had looked up at him, the unexpected visitor, catching her at an employment improbable in a Vicereine. Secretaries or gardeners should have fulfilled this function with which she preferred to deal herself. Her fingers dripping, she had looked up, pushing the hair out of her eyes. But she had pushed something else out of her eyes with the same gesture; she had pushed her whole private life out of them, and had replaced it by the perfunctory courtesy with which she rose, and, giving him her hand, wiping it first on a duster, said, 'Oh, Mr FitzGeorge,' – she had known his name then, temporarily – 'do forgive me, I had no idea it was so late.'

Down in St James's Street, Mr FitzGeorge's frequent absences were noticed. Kay Holland himself observed that Fitz was now less readily available for dinner than formerly, though the explanation lay beyond the wildest range of his suspicion. Far from coming near to the truth, he was full of an undeserved solicitude for his old friend, wondering whether perhaps fatigue or even ill-health compelled him to betake himself early to bed; but on so ceremonious a basis had their relationship always been placed that Kay could venture on no inquiries. He was acquainted with Mr FitzGeorge's rooms and could form some idea of how the old gentleman lived; could, in fact, imagine him shuffling about in a dressing-gown and slippers among the disorder of his incomparable works of art, dissolving a soup-tablet for his supper over the gas-ring, economising the electric light so that one bulb alone illuminated the small Jaeger-clad figure and touched the gilding on the stacked-up frames – or did he resort to a candle-end stuck into a bottle? Kay was sure that Mr FitzGeorge did not allow himself enough to eat, nor could it be very healthy to live among so much dust in the low, over-crowded rooms where a daily charwoman was permitted only the minimum of service. How Fitz himself contrived to emerge presently spruce and well-groomed from this sordid confusion was a mystery to Kay, who spent a great deal of his time in keeping his own surroundings as shiningly clean as possible. No spinster, in fact, could be more house-proud than Kay Holland supervising his annual spring-cleaning; washing, with his shirt-sleeves rolled up, the more fragile of his treasures with his own hands in a basin of water. But old Fitz! Kay supposed that those two rooms had never been turned out since Fitz had moved into them, untold years ago; a magpie's nest under the eaves of Bernard Street, filled with the accumulation carried in, piece by piece; dumped on a chair or on the floor when the chairs gave out, stuffed into a drawer, crowded into a cupboard that would no longer shut; never touched, never dusted, except when Mr FitzGeorge consenting to reveal his masterpieces to a visitor would blow the grimy coating away and hold picture, bronze, or carving up to the light.

And now Fitz was seldom to be seen. When he did walk into the Club, he seemed the same as usual and Kay's misgivings dwindled; if anything, he seemed a little more lively than before, abusing Kay with greater gusto, a twinkle in his eye as though he were enjoying a secret joke. Which indeed he was. Kay sat there, warmed and happy. No one had ever made fun of him as FitzGeorge made fun. But although Kay longed to revert to that conversation about having been seen in his cradle, shyness and habit forbade.

Fitz, however, had ceased asking to be introduced to Lady Slane, much to Kay's relief. He had been sure that his mother would not at all welcome the advent of a stranger in her retirement at Hampstead. He flattered himself, indeed, on his perception in this matter and on the skill he had shown in staving old Fitz off. Yet from time to time he felt a qualm: had he perhaps been rather unkindly firm in discouraging Fitz's one attempt at a new friendship? It must have cost Fitz a great effort to make the suggestion; an even greater effort to renew it. Still, his first duty was to his mother. Neither Carrie, nor Herbert, nor Charles could understand their mother's desire for retirement; but he, Kay, could understand it. It was, therefore, his duty to protect his mother in her desire. He had protected her – though he was usually overawed by Fitz – and thanks to his evasiveness Fitz had apparently forgotten all about his whim. Kay thought that he must go and see his mother one of these days and tell her how clever he had been.

He kept on putting off the expedition, however, for the January weather was bitterly cold, and Kay, who loved warmth and snugness as much as a cat, easily persuaded himself that draughty Underground stations were no place for a coddled person of his advancing years. Well wrapped up in overcoat and muffler, he could just undertake the walk from his rooms in the Temple across Fountain Court, through pigeons too fat to get out of his way, down the steps to the Embankment, up Northumberland Avenue and then through the Park to St James's Street, his daily constitutional, but farther abroad than that he would not venture. He walked, not only for the sake of exercise, but because he had a lively sense of the presence of microbes in all public conveyances; a microbe to him was a horror even greater than a reptile; he seldom got through the day without imagining himself the victim of at least one deadly disease, and never drank a cup of tea without remembering thankfully that the water had been boiled into immunity. As it was, he welcomed a day of rain or sleet which gave him a pretext for remaining indoors. He quieted his conscience by writing little friendly notes to his mother, saying that he had had a cold, that he understood a great deal of influenza was about, and that he hoped Genoux was taking proper care of her. All the same, he thought, on the first fine day he must go to Hampstead and tell his mother about FitzGeorge. She would be amused. She would be grateful.

But Kay, like many a wiser man, deferred his plan just a little too long. He had forgotten Mr FitzGeorge's twenty-five years of seniority. Eighty-one was not an age which permitted the playing of tricks with time. At twenty, thirty, forty, fifty, sixty, one might reasonably say, I will put that off until next summer – though, to be sure, even at twenty, the unexpected perils of life were always present – but at eighty-one such deferments became a mere taunt in the face of Fate. That which had been an unexpected and improbable peril in earlier years, swelled to a certainty after eighty. Kay's standards were perhaps distorted by the longevity of his own family. Certainly FitzGeorge's death came to him as a shock which he received with incredulity and resentment.

The first indication he had of it appeared on the posters: DEATH OF WEST-END CLUB-MAN. He registered this piece of news unconsciously as he walked down the Embankment and turned up Northumberland Avenue on his way to luncheon; it meant no more to him than the news of an omnibus mounting the pavement in Brixton. A little farther on he saw other posters, lunch edition: LONELY MILLIONAIRE DIES IN WEST-END. If the thought of FitzGeorge crossed his mind, he dismissed it; for Bernard Street, even by a journalist, could scarcely be described as West End. Kay had no experience of Fleet Street. Still, he bought a paper. He crossed the Park, noticing that the crocuses were beginning to show green noses above the ground. Thus had he walked a thousand times. Serene, he turned into Boodle's and ordered his bottle of Vichy water, unfolded his napkin, propped the *Evening Standard* before him, and started on his lunch – a cut from the joint, and pickles. He had no need to tell the waiter what he wanted, so regular and recurrent was daily life. There it was, in the second column on the front page: WEST-END CLUB-MAN FOUND DEAD: STRANGE LIFE-STORY OF WEALTHY RECLUSE REVEALED. (Even then, it occurred to Kay to wonder how one could be both a club-man and a recluse.) Then the name hit him: Mr FitzGeorge . . .

He put down his knife and fork with a clatter on his plate so that the other lunchers, who had wondered at Kay Holland's impassivity, raised their heads and whispered: 'Ah, he's heard!' Heard, when they meant read. But indeed with some justice they might say heard, since the printed name had screamed at Kay loud enough to deafen him. He felt as though someone had fetched him a box on the ear. 'Fitz dead?' he said to the man at the next table – a man he did not know, except by sight for the last twenty years, and to whom he had been accustomed to nod.

Then without knowing how he got there, except for some dim recollection of plunging into his pockets to pay the taxi, he found himself in Bernard Street, climbing the stairs to Fitz's rooms. The door into Fitz's rooms was broken in – smashed – splintered – and the police were there, two large young men, pompous and apologetic, very civil and accommodating to Kay when they learnt his name. Fitz was there too, lying on his bed in his Jaeger dressing-gown, curiously stiff. On the table were a sardine and a half, and a half-eaten piece of toast and the remains of a boiled egg, as unappetising as only the cold remains of a boiled egg can be. Fitz wore a night-cap, which was a surprise to Kay, a night-cap with a sideways tassel. He looked much the same as he had looked in life, except that he looked completely different. It was hard to say where the difference came in; the rigidity could scarcely account for it; perhaps it might be attributed to the guilty sense of eavesdropping on old Fitz, of catching him transfixed in a moment hitherto unseen by all eyes, the slippered moment, the nightcap moment, the moment when the three last sardines had been taken from the cupboard. 'We mustn't remove him, sir,' said one of the young policemen, on the watch lest Kay should go too near and touch his friend, 'before the doctors is entirely satisfied.'

Kay shrank towards the window, contrasting this death with

that of his own father. They had indeed chosen very different paths in life. Fitz had scorned the world, he had lived secretly and privately, finding his pleasures within himself, betraying himself to none. Only once had Kay seen him roused, when some newspaper published an article on the eccentrics of London. 'God!' he had said, 'is it eccentric to keep oneself apart?' He had been enraged by the inclusion of his own name. He could see no reason for the curiosity commonly displayed by people over other people; it seemed to him vulgar, boring, and unnecessary. All he asked was to be let alone; he had no desire to interfere in the workings of the world; he simply wanted to live withdrawn into his chosen world, absorbed in his possessions and their beauty. That was his form of spirituality, his form of contemplation. Thus the loneliness of his death held no pathos, since it was in accordance with what he had chosen.

But it worried the agents of the law and the State. They invaded his room, while Kay stood wretchedly by the window fingering the grimy curtains. This gentleman, they said, looking at the stiff and silent figure, had been extremely wealthy; in fact, it was reported that his fortune had run into seven numbers. And although they were accustomed to deal with the lonely death of paupers, no precedent told them how to deal with the lonely death of a millionaire. He must have had *some* relatives, they said, looking at Kay as though Kay were to blame. But Kay said no; so far as he knew, Mr FitzGeorge had no relatives at all; no link with anyone on earth. 'Stay,' he added, 'the South Kensington Museum might be able to tell you something about him.'

At that the Inspector guffawed, and then put his hand over his mouth, remembering that he was in a death-chamber. A museum! he said; well, that was a pretty dreary source of information to go to about a man after he was dead. The Inspector doubtless had a comfortable wife, rows of rowdy children, and pots of red geranium on the window-sill. As a matter of fact, he said, Mr Holland wasn't so far off the mark when he mentioned the Museum. But for the Museum, he, the Inspector, and his subordinates wouldn't be there at all. The presence of the police was most irregular, where there was no suggestion of murder or suicide. Only, thanks to the Museum ringing up Scotland Yard in what the Inspector described as a 'state,' had Scotland Yard sent police to Bernard Street to keep watch over valuable objects which might turn out to be a legacy to the nation. Much as the Inspector manifestly despised the objects, he responded with instant appreciation to the word valuable. But couldn't Mr Holland suggest anything a bit more human than a museum? Mr Holland couldn't. He suggested feebly that they might look Mr FitzGeorge up in *Who's Who.*

Well, said the Inspector, getting out a notebook and settling down to business, who was his father, anyway? Keep those reporters out, he added angrily to his two subordinates. He never had a father, said Kay, feeling like a netted rabbit and wishing that he had never come near Bernard Street to be bullied by the officials of the law. He had, moreover, a suspicion that the Inspector was exceeding his duties in the interest of his curiosity by thus inquiring into the antecedents of the dead millionaire.

The Inspector stared, and a joke dawned in his eyes, but because of his self-importance he suppressed it. 'His mother, then?' he said, implying that although a man might have dispensed with a father he could scarcely dispense with a mother. But Kay had passed beyond the region of such implications; he could see FitzGeorge only as an isolated figure, fighting to maintain its independence. 'He never had a mother either,' he replied.

'Then what *did* he have?' asked the Inspector, glancing at

his subordinates with an expression that summed Kay up in the sole word, Balmy.

Kay was tempted to reply, A private life; for he felt a little light-headed, and the discrepancy between FitzGeorge and the Inspector, with all that the Inspector stood for, was almost too much for him; but he compromised, and pointing to the jumble of works of art cluttering the room, said, 'These.'

'That's not enough,' said the Inspector.

'It was enough for him,' said Kay.

'That junk?' said the Inspector. Kay was silent.

One of the policemen came forward and whispered, showing the Inspector a card. 'All right,' said the Inspector after looking at the card; 'let him in.'

'There's a lot of reporters on the landing, sir, as well.'

'Keep them out, I told you.'

'They say they only want a peep at the room, sir.'

'Well, they can't have it. Tell them there's nothing to see.'

'Very good, sir.'

'Only a lot of junk.'

'Very good, sir.'

'Show in the gentleman from the Museum. Nobody else. It seems,' said the Inspector, turning to Kay, 'that we were right about this here Museum. Here it is, turning up as it might be an uncle of the corpse. Prompt.' He passed the card over to Kay, who read: 'Mr Christopher Foljambe, Victoria and Albert Museum.'

A young man in a bowler-hat, a blue overcoat, kid-gloves, and horn-rimmed spectacles came in. He cast one glance at Mr FitzGeorge and then averted his eyes, which roamed instead over the litter in the room, appraising, while he talked to the Inspector. His attitude, however, differed from the Inspector's, for every now and then his eye would light up and his hand would start out in an involuntary predatory movement towards some dusty but invaluable pile on chair or table. He had, more-over, greeted Kay Holland with deference, thereby increasing Kay's prestige in the Inspector's estimation. A museum, after all, was a public institution, authorised in a very practical (although meagre) way by Government subsidy; and that was the kind of thing which commanded, one might almost say bought, the Inspector's respect. He treated Mr Foljambe with more deference than he had shown to Kay Holland. For in Kay Holland he had not recognised an ex-Prime Minister's son, whereas Mr Foljambe had sent in a card definitely stating: 'Victoria and Albert Museum.'

Mr Foljambe, to do him justice, was ill-at-ease. He had been dispatched by his superiors in a hurry to see that old Fitz's things were duly safeguarded. The Museum, thanks to hints thrown out by old Fitz during the past forty years, considered that they might reasonably expect to have a claim on his possible legacies. Kay Holland, again retreating to the window and again fingering the grimy curtains, gave to both the Inspector and to Mr Foljambe the credit due to them. The Inspector had a duty to fulfil; and Mr Foljambe had been dispatched by his museum on an uncongenial job. Old Fitz's delight in a new discovery, old Fitz's grumpy and restrained rapture over some lovely object, belonged to a different world than this practical protection of a dead man, than this interest in the dead man's dispositions. Kay knew just enough of the world to realise that it must be so. Even on behalf of his friend, he could feel no real irony. The Inspector and Mr Foljambe were both acting according to their lights. And Mr Foljambe, especially, was being very decent about it.

'Of course, I know we have no right to interfere,' he was saying, 'but considering the immense value of the collection, and considering the fact that Mr FitzGeorge always gave us to understand that he would bequeath the majority of his possessions to the nation, my museum felt that some adequate steps should be taken for the safeguarding of the property. I was instructed to say that if you would like one of our men to take charge, he would be at your disposal.'

'Did I understand you to say, sir, that the collection was of immense value?'

'It runs into millions, I should say,' replied Mr Foljambe with relish.

'Well . . .' said the Inspector. 'I don't know anything about such things myself. The room looks to me like a pawnbroker's shop. But if you say so, sir, I must take your word for it. The gentleman,' he jerked his thumb at Mr FitzGeorge, 'appears to have had no family?'

'None that I ever heard of.'

'Very unusual, sir. Very unusual for such a wealthy man.'

'Solicitors?' suggested Mr Foljambe.

'No firm has come forward as yet, sir. Yet the news was in the lunch edition of the papers; true, there's no telephone here,' said the Inspector, looking round in disgust. 'They'd have to come in person.'

'Mr FitzGeorge was a retiring sort of man.'

'So I understand, sir – a real solitary, you might say. Can't understand it myself; I like a bit of company. All right up here, sir?' asked the Inspector, tapping his forehead.

'A bit eccentric perhaps; nothing more.'

'You would expect a gentleman of his sort to be a J.P., or something, wouldn't you, sir? To have some public work, I mean – hospital committees, or something.'

'I don't think Mr FitzGeorge was very publicly minded,' said Mr Foljambe in such a tone that Kay could not decide whether he was being sympathetic or censorious. 'And yet,' he added, 'I oughtn't to say that about a man who can leave such a priceless collection to the nation.'

'You don't know for sure that he has,' said the Inspector.

Mr Foljambe shrugged. 'His hints were pretty clear. And if he hasn't left it to the nation, who could he leave it to? Unless he's left it all to you, Mr Holland,' he said, turning to Kay, pleased by his own joke.

But Mr FitzGeorge had left his collection neither to the nation nor to Kay Holland. He had left it all, including the whole of his fortune, to Lady Slane. The will was written on a half-sheet of paper, but it was perfectly lucid, perfectly in order, duly witnessed, and left no loophole for other interpretation. It revoked a previous will, by which the fortune went to charity and the collection to be divided between various museums and the National and Tate Galleries. It stated expressly that Lady Slane's possession was to be absolute, and that no obligation was imposed on her as to the ultimate disposal.

This news was made public amid general consternation. The rage and dismay of the museums were equalled only by the astonishment and delight of Lady Slane's own family, which gathered at once and in force round Carrie's tea-table. Carrie was in the strong and enviable position of having seen her mother that very afternoon; she had, in fact, rushed straight up to Hampstead. 'Dear Mother,' she said, 'I couldn't leave her alone with that great responsibility thrust upon her. You know how little fitted she is to deal with that kind of thing.' 'But how on earth,' said Herbert, particularly explosive that day, 'how on earth did it all come about? How did she know this man FitzGeorge? And what had Kay to do with it? We know Kay and FitzGeorge were friends; we never knew that Mother knew him so much as by sight. I never heard her mention his name.' Herbert's explosiveness crackled like a heath fire.

'It was a plot, that's what it was; and Kay was at the bottom of it. Kay wanted the old man's things for himself. Well, Kay at any rate has been nicely sold.'

'But has he?' said Charles. 'How do we know that Kay hasn't got some private arrangement with Mother? Kay always kept himself apart from us; I always felt that Kay might be a little unscrupulous.'

'Oh, surely,' began Mabel.

'Be quiet, Mabel,' said Herbert. 'I agree with Charles; certainly Kay has always been a bit of a dark horse. And Mother has never said anything to any of us about her will.'

'Up to now,' said Edith, who had joined her relations, though she despised herself for doing so, 'she has never had anything to leave.'

Edith's remark passed unnoticed as usual.

'I disagree with all of you,' said William, who was respected in his family for having the best grasp of practical considerations; 'if Kay and Mother had had an understanding between them, they would not have arranged for this FitzGeorge's fortune to go first to Mother. Think of the duties.'

'Death-duties?' said Edith, tactless as usual, uttering the unpleasant word.

'Half a million at least,' said William. 'No. Much better that it should all have gone straight to Kay.'

'But Mother is so unpractical,' said Carrie with a sigh.

'Tragically unpractical,' said William. 'Why didn't she consult one of us? But it's done now,' he resumed more philosophically, 'and what in Heaven's name will she do with it all?'

'She seemed to take no interest in it,' said Carrie. 'I found her reading a book while Genoux fed scraps to the cat in the corner. I don't believe she was really reading it, for when I asked her the title – just trying to make conversation, you know – she couldn't tell me. She said it was something Mudie had sent, but, as you know, Mother always makes up her lists most carefully, and never leaves it to Mudie. I had some difficulty in getting in, because, it appears, the house had been so besieged by newspaper men that Mother had forbidden Genoux to answer the door-bell. I had to go round into the garden and shout "Mother!" under the window.'

'Well,' said Herbert, as Carrie paused, 'and when you had got in, what explanation did she give you?'

'None. She had known this FitzGeorge in India, it appears, and he had been to call on her once or twice recently. So she told me. But I am sure she was keeping something back. When she said FitzGeorge had been to call on her, Genoux, who was hovering about, began to cry and went out of the room. She picked up her apron and began to sniff into it. As she went she said something about "Un si gentil monsieur." From which I assume that he had always given her a tip.'

'And what about Mother? Did she seem upset?'

'She was quiet,' said Carrie after a pause, judicially. 'Yes, on the whole, I'm sure she was keeping something back. She kept trying to change the subject. As though one could change the subject! She hadn't seen the posters in London; that was evident. Dear Mother, I was only trying to help her. I did feel it was a little hard to be so misunderstood. She seemed to want to keep me out of it – to keep me at arm's length.'

'But,' said Lavinia, 'what could one want to keep back, at your mother's age? Not . . . ?'

'Well,' said Carrie, 'one never knows, does one?'

'No,' said Herbert, 'no! I can't believe *that*!' He spoke righteously, as the head of the family.

'Perhaps not,' said Carrie, deferring to him; 'I'm sure your judgment is best, Herbert. And yet, you know, a very strange idea struck me.'

They all edged forward to hear Carrie's very strange idea.

'No, I really can't say it,' said Carrie, delighted at having aroused so much interest; 'I really can't, not even here where I know it would go no further.'

'Carrie!' said Herbert, 'you know we always had a pact that we would never start a sentence unless we meant to finish it.'

'When we were children,' said Carrie, keeping up her reluctance.

'Of course, if you would rather not . . .' said Herbert.

'Well, if you insist,' said Carrie. 'This is what struck me. None of us ever knew of Mother's friendship with this old man – this old FitzGeorge. She never mentioned him to any of us. Now it turns out that she knew him in India – just about the time when Kay was born – perhaps before. And he always took an interest in Kay. Then he dies, leaving everything to Mother – not to Kay, it's true. But that's no reason why Mother shouldn't leave it all in turn to Kay. And perhaps he always meant Kay to have it. He merely short-circuited Kay. Who knows that that may not have been a kind of bluff? Eccentric old men like that, you know, are always terrified of scandal.'

'Because . . .' said Herbert.

'Exactly. Because.'

'Oh no, no!' said Edith, 'it's horrible, Carrie, it's monstrous. Mother loved Father, she never would have deceived him.'

'Dear Edith!' said Carrie. 'So naïve! seeing everything in terms of black or white!' But already she regretted having spoken in the presence of Edith, who might betray her to their mother. She had the best of reasons for wishing to remain on good terms with her mother at present.

Edith took her departure in indignation, leaving a united family behind her. They drew their chairs a little closer.

'And then,' said Carrie, going on with her story, 'a young man came – a most unpleasant young man. Foljambe, from

146

some museum. Genoux behaved most unsuitably. I suppose that he had given her his card, instead of merely giving her his name; anyway, she announced him as Monsieur Follejambe. I suspect that she did it on purpose. But I soon saw that it served him right. It was quite clear that he and his museum had designs on poor Mother's inheritance. He pretended that he had come with an offer from his museum to house the collection if Mother hadn't room for it. Mother, for once, was quite sensible. She would make no promises. She said she hadn't decided what to do. She looked at Foljambe as though he weren't there. And then, of course, Genoux burst in as she always does, asking whether Mother would rather have cutlets or a chicken for dinner. A chicken, she said, was less economical, but it could be finished up next day. And Mother with at least eighty thousand a year!'

Lavinia groaned.

'But Mother was just as reticent with me as with the young man,' Carrie continued. 'I kept on assuring her that I only wanted to help – and you all know me well enough to believe that that was the simple truth – but she looked at me just as vaguely as she looked at Foljambe. She seemed to be thinking of something else all the time. Sentimental memories, perhaps,' said Carrie viciously. 'She didn't even ask me to stay to dinner, when Genoux came in again to say the chicken was nearly ready and would spoil. I had to leave with Foljambe finally, and, of course, I had to offer him a lift in the car. He tells me that the collection, apart from the fortune, is estimated at a couple of million.'

'Poor Father,' said Herbert; 'for the first time I feel glad that he is no longer alive.'

'Yes, that's a great comfort,' said Carrie. 'Poor Father. He never knew.'

They silently digested this comforting fact.

'But,' said William, ever practical, resuming the conversation, 'what will Mother do with all those things – all that money? Eighty thousand a year! And two million or so locked up in works of art! Why, if she sold them, she'd have a hundred and sixty thousand a year – more, if she invested it at five per cent. As she easily could.' His voice became shrill, as it always did over any question of money. 'One never knows, with Mother. Look at the casual way she behaved over the jewels. She seems to have no idea of value, no idea of responsibility. For all we know, she may hand over the whole collection to the nation.'

Terror descended upon Lady Slane's family.

'You don't really believe that, William? Surely she must have *some* feeling for her children?'

'I do believe it,' said William, working himself up. 'Mother is like a child who treats rubies as though they were pebbles. She has never learnt; she has merely wandered through life. You know we have always tacitly felt that Mother wasn't quite like other people. One doesn't like to say that sort of thing about one's mother, but at moments like this one can't afford to be over-delicate. At any moment she may do something erratic, something which makes one wring one's hands in despair. And we are powerless. Powerless!'

'Nonsense, William,' said Carrie, feeling that William was dramatising the situation; 'Mother has always been amenable to reason.'

'Even when she went to live at Hampstead?' said William gloomily. 'I can't agree that people who strike out a new line for themselves at Mother's age are amenable to reason. Even when she gave away the jewels in that ridiculous way?' He looked at Mabel, who nervously tried to cover up the pearls by some stringy lace. 'No, Carrie. Mother is a person who has never had her feet on the ground. Cloud-cuckoo-land – that's

Mother's natural home. And, unfortunately, she has met with another inhabitant: Mr FitzGeorge.'

'And what about Bucktrout?' said Carrie.

'What, indeed?' said William. 'Bucktrout may well induce her to make the whole fortune over to him. Poor Mother – so simple, so unwise. A prey. What is to be done?'

Meanwhile, Mr Bucktrout had called on Lady Slane to condole with her over this sudden responsibility.

'You see, Mr Bucktrout,' said Lady Slane, who was looking ill and troubled, 'Mr FitzGeorge couldn't have known what he was doing. He wanted me to enjoy his beautiful things – I realise that. But what did he imagine I could do with so much money? I have quite enough for my wants. I knew a millionaire once, Mr Bucktrout, and he was the most unhappy of men. He was so much afraid of assassination that he lived surrounded by detectives. They were like mice in the walls. He wouldn't allow himself to make a friend, because he couldn't get ulterior motives out of his mind. When one sat beside him at dinner, he was all the time fearing that one would end by asking him for a subscription to a favourite charity. Most people disliked him. I liked him very much. I have seen a great deal of men who mistrusted others because they scented ulterior motives, Mr Bucktrout, and I don't want to be put into the same position. It seems absurd that Mr FitzGeorge, of all men, should have put me into it. I don't think he can have known what he was doing.'

'In the eyes of the world, Lady Slane,' said Mr Bucktrout, 'Mr FitzGeorge has conferred an enormous benefit upon you.'

'I know, I know,' said Lady Slane, deeply worried and distressed, and not wishing to appear ungrateful.

All her life long, she was thinking, people had conferred benefits on her, benefits she did not covet. Henry by making her first into a Vicereine, and then into a political hostess, and now FitzGeorge by heaping her quiet life with gold and treasures.

'I never wanted anything, Mr Bucktrout,' she said, 'but to stand aside. One of the things, it appears, that the world doesn't allow! Even at the age of eighty-eight.'

'Even the smallest planet,' said Mr Bucktrout sententiously, 'is compelled to circle round the sun.'

'But does that mean,' asked Lady Slane, 'that we must all, willy-nilly, circle round wealth, position, possessions? I thought Mr FitzGeorge knew better. Don't *you* understand?' she said, appealing to Mr Bucktrout in desperation. 'I thought I had escaped at last from all those things, and now Mr FitzGeorge, of all people, pushes me back into the thick of them. What am I to do, Mr Bucktrout? What am I to do? I believe Mr FitzGeorge collected very beautiful things, but I know nothing of such things. I always preferred the works of God to the works of man. The works of God, I always felt, were given freely to anyone who could appreciate them, whether millionaire or pauper, whereas the works of man were reserved for the millionaires. Unless, indeed, the works of man were sufficient to the man who made them; then, it wouldn't matter what millionaire bought them in after years. Not that Mr FitzGeorge,' she added, 'bought the works of man because of their value. He was an artist in appreciation. Besides, he was a miser. Far from paying the market value of a work of art, it amused him to discover a work of art for less than its market value. Then he felt he had got it on terms of a work of God rather than a work of man, if you follow me.'

'I follow you perfectly,' said Mr Bucktrout.

'Few people would,' said Lady Slane. 'You encourage me to think that you sympathise with my position as few people would sympathise. I don't want all these valuable things, beautiful though they may be. It would worry me to think that I had upon my mantelpiece a terra-cotta Cellini, which Genoux would certainly break, dusting one morning before breakfast. No, Mr Bucktrout. I would rather go up on to the Heath, if I want something to look at, and look at Constable's trees.'

'Rather than own a Constable?' asked Mr Bucktrout shrewdly. 'I believe that Mr FitzGeorge's collection includes a very fine Constable of Hampstead Heath.'

'Well,' said Lady Slane, relaxing, 'I might perhaps keep that.'

'But for the rest, Lady Slane,' said Mr Bucktrout, 'excluding a few pieces that you might be willing to keep for personal reasons, what shall you decide to do?'

'Give them away,' said Lady Slane wearily, not energetically. 'Let the nation have them. Let the hospitals have the money. As Mr FitzGeorge first intended. Let me be rid of it all. Only let me be rid of it! Besides,' she added, with the twist to which Mr Bucktrout had become accustomed, 'think how much I shall annoy my children!'

He fully appreciated the subtlety of the practical joke that Lady Slane was playing on her children. Practical jokes, in principle, did not amuse Mr Bucktrout; he dismissed them as childish and silly; but this particular joke tickled his sense of humour. He had formed a shrewd idea of Lady Slane's children, although he had never seen them.

'But when you die,' said Mr Bucktrout, with his usual forthrightness, 'your obituary notices will point to you as a disinterested benefactor of the public.'

'I shan't be there to read them,' said Lady Slane, who had learnt enough from Lord Slane's obituary notices about the possibilities of false interpretation.

Mr Bucktrout walked away genuinely concerned with the

perplexity of his old friend. It never occurred to him that most people would regard Lady Slane's wistful regrets as very peculiar regrets indeed. He accepted quite simply the fact that Lady Slane disagreed with the world's customary values, and accordingly it seemed natural to him that she should resent having them so constantly forced upon her. Moreover, he now knew all about her early ambitions, and their complete variance with her actual life. Mr Bucktrout, although simple in many ways – most people thought him a little mad – was also endowed with a direct and unprejudiced wisdom of his own: he knew that standards must be altered to fit the circumstances, and that it was absurd, although usual, to expect the circumstances to adjust themselves to ready-made standards. Lady Slane thus, in his opinion, deserved as much sympathy in the frustration of her life as an athlete stricken with paralysis. It was an unconventional view to take, no doubt, but Mr Bucktrout never questioned its rightness.

Genoux, however, was struck with horror when she heard what Lady Slane proposed to do. Her French soul was appalled. For a couple of days she had walked on air, and in order to celebrate this sudden, this unbelievable, accretion of wealth had bought some extra pieces of fish for the cat. Her ideas of the fortune bequeathed to Lady Slane – she had read the amount in the papers, and had counted the zeros on her fingers, incredulously doing the sum several times over – were curiously mixed: she knew well enough what a million was, what two millions were, but in practical application she decided only that she might now venture to ask Lady Slane for the charwoman three times a week instead of twice. Hitherto, in the interests of economy, she had not spared herself even when her rheumatism made her stiffer than usual. She had simply doubled her coverings of brown paper, had put on an extra petticoat, and gone about her business hoping for relief. She knew miladi was not rich, and would rather suffer herself than add to miladi's expenses. But with Lady Slane's decision, casually communicated to her one evening as she came to remove the tray, all visions of future extravagance vanished. 'C'est pas possible, miladi!' she exclaimed. 'Et moi qui pensais voir revenir nos plus beaux jours!' Genoux was really in despair. Moreover, she had been delighted by the light of publicity turned once more on Lady Slane. Both the daily papers and the weekly illustrated papers had flaunted Lady Slane's photograph; the photographs had been very out-of-date, it was true, since nothing recent was available; they had shown Lady Slane as Vicereine, as Ambassadress, young, bejewelled, in evening dress, a tiara crowning her elaborate *coiffure*, seated under a palm; curiously old-fashioned; holding an open book in which she was not reading; surrounded by her children, Herbert in his sailor suit, Carrie in her party frock – how well Genoux remembered it! – leaning affectionately over their mother's shoulders, looking down at the baby – was it Charles? was it William? – she held upon her knee. One paper even, accepting the impossibility of getting a photograph of Lady Slane to-day, had boldly made the best of a bad job and had reproduced a photograph taken in her wedding dress seventy years ago. The companion picture was of Lord Slane in jodhpurs, rifle in hand, one foot resting on a tiger. These things, which Lady Slane so inexplicably did not like, satisfied Genoux's sense of fitness. It was not for her to dictate to miladi, she said, but had miladi considered her position and what was due to it? miladi, who had been accustomed to all those aides-de-camp, all those servants – 'bien que ce n'était que des nègres' – all those orderlies, ready to run at any moment with a note or a message? 'Dans ce temps-là, miladi était au moins bien servie.' Then, in the midst of her despair, a thought struck Genoux which caused her to double up suddenly and rub her hands up and down her thighs. 'Ah, mon Dieu, miladi, c'est Lady Charlotte qui va être contente! Et Monsieur William, donc! Ah, la belle plaisanterie!'

Lady Slane was lonely, now that Mr FitzGeorge had gone. The excitement aroused by her gift to the nation, and the frenzy displayed by her own children, all passed over her without making much impression. She forbade Genoux to bring a newspaper into the house until the headlines should have dwindled to a mere paragraph, and she refused to see any of her children until they would consent to treat the matter as though it had never happened. Carrie wrote a carefully composed and dignified letter; a few weeks, possibly even a few months must elapse, she said, before this terrible wound could heal sufficiently to allow her to observe her mother's condition of silence. Until then she could not trust herself. When she had recovered a little she would write again. Meanwhile it was clear that Lady Slane must consider herself in the direst disgrace.

But although this left her unmoved, and although, thanks to Kay and to Mr Bucktrout, she had had very little trouble with the authorities, beyond appending her signature to a few documents, she felt tired now and emptied in spirit. Her friendship with FitzGeorge had been strange and lovely – the last strange and lovely thing that was ever likely to happen to her. She desired nothing more. She desired only peace and the laying-down of vexation.

From time to time she came across allusions to her family in the papers. Carrie had opened a bazaar. Carrie's granddaughter was taking part in a charity matinée. Charles had succeeded in getting one of his letters into *The Times*. Richard – Herbert's eldest grandson – had won a point-to-point race. Deborah, his sister, had become most suitably engaged to the eldest son of a duke. Herbert himself had been delivered of a speech in the House of Lords. It was rumoured that the next vacant Governor-generalship would be awarded to Herbert. As it was, he had received the K.C.M.G. in the New Year Honours ... From the immense distance of her years Lady Slane contemplated these happenings, tiny and far-off, bringing with them some echo of the events mixed up with her own life. 'How weary, flat, stale, and unprofitable,' she said to herself, going carefully downstairs with the help of a stick and the banisters, and wondering why, at the end of one's life, one should ever trouble to read anything but Shakespeare; or, for the matter of that, at the beginning of one's life either, since he seemed to have understood both exuberance and maturity. But it was only in maturity, perhaps, that one could fully appreciate his deeper understanding.

She looked upon this group of people, sprung from her own loins, and saw them in mid-career or else starting out upon their course. Young Deborah, she supposed, was happy in her engagement, and young Richard felt himself filled to the brim with life as he rode across country. She smiled quite tenderly as she thought of the two young creatures. But they would harden, she thought, they would harden when their warm youth grew chilled; they would become worldly-wise, self-seeking; the rash generosity of youth would be replaced by the prudence of middle-age. There would be no battle for them, no struggle in their souls; they would simply set hard into the moulds prepared for them. Lady Slane sighed to think that she was responsible, though indirectly, for their existence. The long, weary serpent of posterity streamed away from her. She felt sick at heart, and looked forward only to release.

Still, she did an inexplicable thing. After she had done it – after she had written the letter, stamped it, and given it to

Genoux to post – she looked back upon her action and decided that she had acted in a trance. She could not say what impulse had moved her, what strange desire had tugged at her to recreate a link with the life she had abjured. Perhaps her loneliness was greater than any human courage could stand; perhaps she had overrated her own fortitude. Only a very strong soul could stand quite alone. Be that as it might, she had written to a press-cutting agency with the instruction that any references to her own family should be supplied to her. Privately, she knew that she wanted only the references to her great-grandchildren. She cared very little what happened to Carrie, Herbert, Charles, and William; the path that they followed and would continue to follow was clearly marked, offering no surprises, no delights. But even in her trance she shrank from betraying herself to the eyes of an agency in Holborn: she disguised her real desire under the extravagance of a general order. When the little green packets began to arrive, however, all references to her own children went straight into the waste-paper basket, and references to her great-grandchildren only were pasted very carefully by Lady Slane into an album bought from the stationer round the corner.

She derived an extraordinary pleasure from this occupation, carried on every evening under the shade of the pink lamp. Every evening, for, realising that a fresh supply would not arrive more than twice or thrice a week, she economised her little hoard, and would allow herself the luxury of pasting in only a proportion of the cuttings every day, so that one or two might always remain left over for the morrow. Fortunately, out of Lady Slane's great-grandchildren, two were grown-up, and their activities manifold. They were, in fact, among the prominent young people of the day, and in the gossip columns they had their news-value. Many pleasant hours were spent by Lady Slane in constructing their characters and personalities from these snippets, reinforced by her previous knowledge of them; a recreation for their great-grandmother of which the children themselves were entirely ignorant, an ignorance which added considerably to Lady Slane's half-mischievous, half-sentimental pleasure, for pleasure to her was entirely a private matter, a secret joke, intense, redolent, but as easily bruised as the petals of a gardenia. Genoux alone knew of her nightly occupation, but Genoux was no intrusion, being as much a part of Lady Slane as her boots or her hot-water bottle, or as the cat John, who sat bunched with incomparable neatness and dignity before the fire. Genoux indeed shared Lady Slane's interest in the young Hollands, though from a different point of view. She had been quick to guess and to welcome Lady Slane's reviving interest, and trotted in with a green packet as soon as it had fallen through the letter-box. 'Voilà, miladi! c'est arrivé!' and she would stand by expectantly while Lady Slane stripped off the wrapper and revealed the print. They were futile enough, heaven knows, these paragraphs. Treasure-hunting in Underground stations; a ball; a party; sometimes a photograph, of Richard in riding-breeches or of Deborah representing Mary Queen of Scots at a fancy-dress ball. Futile, but young and harmless. Lady Slane turned them over, and who should presume to analyse her feelings? But Genoux frankly clasped her hands in ecstasy. 'Ah, miladi, qu'il est donc beau, Monsieur Richard! Ah, miladi, qu'elle est donc jolie!' That was Deborah. Lady Slane would smile, pleased by Genoux's admiration. She was, after all, an old woman, and small things pleased her now. 'Yes,' she said, looking at a photograph of Richard, muddy, holding a silver cup under one arm and a riding whip under the other, 'he is a well-built young man – pas si mal.' 'Pas si mal!' cried Genoux in indignation, 'he is superb, a god; such elegance, such chic. All the young women must be mad about him. And he will follow in the footsteps of his great-grandfather,' added Genoux, who had a wholesome appreciation of worldly prestige; 'he will be Viceroy, Prime Minister, Dieu sait quoi encore; miladi verra.' For Genoux had never estimated Lady Slane's contempt for such things. 'No, Genoux,' said Lady Slane; 'I shan't be there to see.'

She would see only, and at so queer a remove, their lovely, silly youth. Thank God, she would not be there to see their hardening into an even sillier adult life, redeemed not even by this wild, foolish, but decorative quality. 'Nymphs and shepherds, come away,' she murmured, looking at the thick hair, the slim elastic limbs. 'Ah, Genoux,' she said, 'it was good to be young.'

That depends, said Genoux sagely, on what sort of a youth one had. It was not good to be the twelfth child of poor parents, and to be sent to live with farmers near Poitiers; to sleep on straw in a barn; never to see one's parents; to get up at five every morning, winter and summer; to be beaten if one didn't do one's work properly; to know that one's brothers and sisters were growing up as strangers. Genoux had been with Lady Slane for nearly seventy years, yet Lady Slane had never heard this revelation. She turned to Genoux with curiosity. 'And when you did see your brothers and sisters again, Genoux, did it feel very strange to you?'

Not a bit, said Genoux; blood counted. One's own family was one's own family. She had walked into the little flat in Paris, at the age of sixteen, as though she belonged there by right. The farm near Poitiers had vanished, and she never thought of it again, though she knew better than anybody where the straying hens laid their eggs. She had walked straight into the lives of her brothers and sisters and had taken up her place there as though she had never been away. She had had a little trouble with one of her sisters, who had given birth to twins just after her elder child had died of diphtheria. They had tried to conceal the death from her, Genoux said, but she had guessed it somehow, and leaping straight out of bed had rushed as she was, in her nightgown, to the cemetery, there to fling herself upon the grave. Genoux had been sent to fetch her back, nor had it apparently struck her as odd that a girl of her age should be employed on such a mission. Necessity ruled; and her mother had to stay at home to look after the twins. But her sojourn with her family had been but a brief interlude. Her father had already put down her name at a registry office, and the next thing she knew was that she was crossing the Channel to England, to take service with miladi.

Lady Slane listened with some emotion to this simple and philosophical recital. She blamed herself for never having questioned Genoux before. She had taken Genoux for granted, all these years; yet a wealth of experience was locked up in that sturdy breast. It must have been a curious transition, from the farm near Poitiers, where she slept on straw and was beaten, to the magnificence of Government House and Viceregal Lodge ... The experiences of her great-grandchildren seemed shallow indeed by comparison; her own experiences seemed thin and over-civilised, lacking any contact with reality. She, who had brooded in secret over an unfulfilled vocation, had never been obliged to tear a distraught sister away from a newly-dug grave. Watching Genoux, who stood there imperturbably relating these trials out of the past, she wondered which wounds went the deeper: the jagged wounds of reality, or the profound invisible bruises of the imagination?

Since those days Genoux had never had any personal life, she supposed. Her life was in her service, with self submerged. Lady Slane suddenly condemned herself as an egoistic old woman. Yet, she reflected, she also had given her life away, to Henry. She need not blame herself overmuch for the last indulgence of her melancholy.

She returned to Genoux. The Holland family had replaced Genoux's own family, absorbing everything that Genoux possessed of pride, ambition, snobbery. She remembered Genoux's paeans of delight when Henry had been given a peerage. Over every child she had watched as though it were her own, and nothing but her fierce protectiveness of Lady Slane could have drawn from her a word of criticism about the Holland children. Now she transferred her interest to the great-grandchildren, making no difference since the day they had ceased to come to the house. Her loyal soul had momentarily been torn in half by Lady Slane's refusal to receive Deborah and Richard. But when Lady Slane explained that youthful vitality was too tiring for an old lady, she had at once readjusted her notions. 'Bien sûr, miladi; la jeunesse, c'est très fatigant.'

She welcomed, however, this suitable revival of family pride typified in the green packets and the album. Deep down in her peasant wisdom, she recognised the wholesome instinct for perpetuation in posterity. Her own womanhood unfulfilled, she clung pathetically to a vicarious satisfaction through the medium of her adored Lady Slane. 'Ça me fait du bien,' she said, tears in her eyes, 'de voir miladi s'occuper avec son petit pot of Stickphast.' And once she lifted up John, the cat, to look at a full-page photograph of Richard in the *Tatler*. 'Regarde, mon bobo, le beau gars.' John struggled and would not look. She set him down again, disappointed. 'C'est drôle, miladi; les animaux, c'est si intelligent, mais ça ne reconnaît jamais les images.'

Common sense rarely laid its fingers on Lady Slane, these days. It did occur to her to wonder, however, what the young people had thought of her renunciation of FitzGeorge's fortune. They had been indignant probably; they had cursed their great-grandmother soundly for defrauding them of a benefit which would eventually have been theirs. They would certainly have given her no credit for romantic motives. Perhaps she owed them an explanation, though not an apology? But how could she get into touch with them, now especially? Pride caught her wrist even as she stretched her pen out towards the ink. She had, after all, behaved towards them in what to any reasonable person must seem a most unnatural way; first she had refused to see them, and then she had eliminated from their future the possibility of great and easy wealth. She must appear to them as the incarnation of egoism and inconsideration. Lady Slane was distressed, yet she knew that she had acted according to her convictions. Had not FitzGeorge himself once taken her to task for sinning against the light? And suddenly, in a moment of illumination, she understood why FitzGeorge had tempted her with this fortune: he had tempted her only in order that she should find the strength to reject it. He had offered her not so much a fortune as a chance to be true to herself. Lady Slane bent down and stroked the cat, whom as a rule she did not much like. 'John,' she said, 'John – how fortunate that I did what he wanted, before I realised what he wanted.'

After that she was happy, though her qualms about her young descendants continued to worry her. By a curious twist, her qualms of conscience about them increased now that she had satisfactorily explained her own action to herself, as though she blamed herself for some extravagant gesture of self-indulgence. Perhaps she had come too hastily to her decision? Perhaps she had treated the children unfairly? Perhaps one should not demand sacrifices of others, consequent upon one's own ideas? She had consulted her own ideas entirely, with the added spice of pleasure, she must admit, in annoying Carrie, Herbert, Charles, and William. It had seemed wrong to her that private people should own such possessions, such exaggerated wealth; therefore she had hastened to dispose of both, the treasures to the public and the money to the suffering poor;

the logic was simple though trenchant. Stated in these terms, she could not believe in her own wrong-doing; but, on the other hand, should she not have considered her great-grandchildren? It was a subtle problem to decide alone; and Mr Bucktrout, to whom she confided it, gave her no help, for not only was he entirely in sympathy with her first instinct but, moreover, in view of the approaching end of the world, he could not see that it mattered very much one way or the other. 'My dear lady,' he said, 'when your Cellinis, your Poussins, your grand-children, and your great-grandchildren are all mingled in planetary dust your problem of conscience will cease to be of much impor-tance.' That was true rather than helpful. Astronomical truths, enlarging though they may be to the imagination, contain little assistance for immediate problems. She continued to gaze at him in distress, a distress which at that very moment had been augmented by a sudden thought of what Henry, raising his eye-brows, would have said.

'Miss Deborah Holland,' said Genoux, throwing open the door. She threw it open in such a way as to suggest that she was retrospectively aping the manner of the grand major-domo at the Paris Embassy.

Lady Slane rose in a fluster, with the usual soft rustle of her silks and laces; her knitting slipped to the floor; she stooped ineffectually to retrieve it; her mind swept wildly round, seek-ing to reconcile this improbable encounter between her great-granddaughter, Mr Bucktrout, and herself. The circum-stances were too complicated for her to govern successfully in a moment's thought. She had never been good at dealing with a situation that demanded nimbleness of wit; and, considering the conversations she had had with Mr Bucktrout about her great-grandchildren, of whom Herbert's granddaughter thus suddenly presented herself as a specimen, the situation demanded a very nimble wit indeed. 'My *dear* Deborah,' said

Lady Slane, scurrying affectionately, dropping her knitting, trying to retrieve it, abandoning the attempt midway, and finally managing to kiss Deborah on the cheek.

She was the more confused, for Deborah was the first young person to enter the house at Hampstead since Lady Slane had removed herself from Elm Park Gardens. The house at Hampstead had opened its doors to no one but Mr FitzGeorge, Mr Bucktrout, and Mr Gosheron – and, of course, on occasion, to Lady Slane's own children, who, although they might be unwelcome, were at any rate advanced in years. Deborah came in the person of youth knocking at the doors. She was pretty, under her fur cap; pretty and elegant; the very girl Lady Slane would have expected from her photographs in the society papers. In the year since Lady Slane had seen her, she had changed from a schoolgirl into a young lady. Of her activities in the fashionable world since she became a young lady, Lady Slane had had ample evidence. This observation reminded Lady Slane of her press-cutting album, which was lying on the table under the lamp; releasing Deborah's hand, she hurriedly removed the album to a dark place, as though it were a dirtied cup of tea. She put the blotter over it. A narrow escape; narrow and unforeseen; but now she felt safe. She came back and introduced Deborah formally to Mr Bucktrout.

Mr Bucktrout had the tact to take his leave almost immediately. Lady Slane, knowing him, had feared that he might plunge instantly into topics of the deepest import, with references to her own recent and eccentric conduct, thereby embarrassing both the girl and herself. Mr Bucktrout, however, behaved most unexpectedly as a man of the world. He made a few remarks about the beginning of spring – about the reappearance of flowers on barrows in the London streets – about the longevity of anemones in water, especially if you cut their stems – about the bunches of snowdrops that came up from the country, and how soon they would be succeeded by bunches of primroses – about Covent Garden. But about cosmic catastrophes or the right judgment of Deborah Holland's great-grandmother he said nothing. Only once did he verge on an indiscretion, when he leant forward, putting his finger against his nose, and said, 'Miss Deborah, you bear a certain resemblance to Lady Slane whom I have the honour to call my friend.' Fortunately, he did not follow up the remark, but after the correct interval merely rose and took his leave. Lady Slane was grateful to him, yet it was with dismay that she saw him go, leaving her face to face with a young woman bearing what had once been her own name.

She expected an evasive and meaningless conversation as a start, dreading the chance phrase that would fire it into realities, growing swiftly like Jack's beanstalk into a tangle of reproaches; she expected anything in the world but that Deborah should sit at her knee and thank her with directness and simplicity for what she had done. Lady Slane made no answer at all, except to lay her hand on the girl's head pressed against her knee. She was too much moved to answer; she preferred to let the young voice go on, imagining that she herself was the speaker, reviving her adolescent years and deluding herself with the fancy that she had at last found a confidant to whom she could betray her thoughts. She was old, she was tired, she lost herself willingly in the sweet illusion. Was it an echo that she heard? or had some miracle wiped out the years? were the years being played over again, with a difference? She allowed her fingers to ruffle Deborah's hair, and, finding it short instead of ringleted, supposed vaguely that she had put her own early plans for escape into execution. Had she then really run away from home? had she, indeed, chosen her own career instead of Henry's? Was she now sitting on the floor beside a trusted friend, pouring out her reasons, her aspirations, and her convictions, with a firmness and a certainty lit as by a flame from within? Fortunate Deborah! she thought, to be so firm, so trustful, and by one person at least so well understood; but to which Deborah she alluded, she scarcely knew.

She had told herself after FitzGeorge's death that no strange and lovely thing would ever enter her life again, a foolish prophecy. This unexpected confusion of her own life with that of her great-granddaughter was as strange and as lovely. FitzGeorge's death had aged her; at her time of life people aged suddenly and alarmingly; her mind was, perhaps, no longer very clear; but at least it was clear enough for her to recognise its weakness, and to say, 'Go on, my darling; you might be myself speaking.' Deborah, in her young egoism, failed to pick up the significance of that remark, which Lady Slane, indeed, had inadvertently let slip. She had no intention of revealing herself to her great-granddaughter; her hand upon the latch of the door of death, she had no intention of troubling the young with a recital of her own past problems; enough for her, now to submerge herself into a listener, a pair of ears, though she might still keep her secrets running in and out of her mind according to her fancy – for it must be remembered that Lady Slane had always relished the privacy of her enjoyments. This enjoyment was especially private now, though not very sharp; it was hazy rather than sharp, her perceptions intensified and yet blurred, so that she could feel intensely without being able or obliged to reason. In the deepening twilight of her life, in the maturity of her years, she returned to the fluctuations of adolescence; she became once more the reed wavering in the river, the skiff reaching out towards the sea, yet blown back again and again into the safe waters of the estuary. Youth! youth! she thought; and she, so near to death, imagined that all the perils again awaited her, but this time she would face them more bravely, she would allow no concessions, she would be firm and certain. This child, this Deborah, this self, this other self, this projection of herself, was firm and certain. Her engagement, she said, was a mistake; she had drifted into it to please her grandfather; (Mother doesn't count, she said, nor does Granny – poor Mabel!) her grandfather had ambitions for her, she said; he liked the idea of her being, some day, a duchess; but what was that, she said, compared with what she herself wanted to be, a musician?

When she said 'a musician,' Lady Slane received a little shock, so confidently had she expected Deborah to say 'a painter.' But it came to much the same thing, and her disappointment was quickly healed. The girl was talking as she herself would have talked. She had no prejudice against marriage with someone who measured his values against the same rod as herself. Understanding was impossible between people who did not agree as to the yard and the inch. To her grandfather and her late fiancé, wealth and so great a title measured a yard – two yards – a hundred yards – a mile. To her, they measured an inch – half an inch. Music, on the other hand, and all that it implied, could be measured by no terrestrial scale. Therefore she was grateful to her great-grandmother for reducing her value in the worldly market. 'You see,' she said amused, 'for a week I was supposed to be an heiress, and when it was found that I wasn't an heiress at all it became much easier for me to break off my engagement.'

'When did you break it off?' asked Lady Slane, thinking of her newspaper cuttings which had not mentioned the fact.

'The day before yesterday.'

Genoux came in with the evening post, glad of a pretext to take another look at Deborah. Lady Slane slipped the green packet under her knitting. 'I didn't know,' she said, 'that you had broken it off.'

And such a relief it was, said Deborah, wriggling her shoulders. She would have no more to do, she said, with that crazy world. 'Is it crazy, great-grandmother,' she asked, 'or am I? Or am I merely one of the people who can't fit in? Am I just one of the people who think a different set of things important? Anyhow, why should I accept other people's ideas? My own are just as likely to be right – right for me. I know one or two people who agree with me, but they are always people who don't seem to get on with grandfather or great-aunt Carrie. And another thing' – she paused.

'Go on,' said Lady Slane, moved to the heart by this stumbling and perplexed analysis.

'Well,' said Deborah, 'there seems to be a kind of solidarity between grandfather and great-aunt Carrie and the people that grandfather and great-aunt Carrie approve of. As though cement had been poured over the whole lot. But the people I like always seem to be scattered, lonely people – only they recognise each other as soon as they come together. They seem to be aware of something more important than the things grandfather and great-aunt Carrie think important. I don't yet know exactly what that something is. If it were religion – if I wanted to become a nun instead of a musician – I think that even grandfather would understand dimly what I was talking about. But it isn't religion; and yet it seems to have something of the nature of religion. A chord of music, for instance, gives me more satisfaction than a prayer.'

'Go on,' said Lady Slane.

'Then,' said Deborah, 'among the people I like, I find something hard and concentrated in the middle of them, harsh, almost cruel. A sort of stone of honesty. As though they were determined at all costs to be true to the things that they think matter. Of course,' said Deborah dutifully, remembering the comments of her grandfather and her great-aunt Carrie, 'I know that they are, so to speak, very useless members of society.' She said it with a childish gravity.

'They have their uses,' said Lady Slane; 'they act as a leaven.'

'I never know how to pronounce that word,' said Deborah; 'whether to rhyme with even or seven. I suppose you are right about them, great-grandmother. But the leaven takes a long time to work, and even then it only works among people who are more or less of the same mind.'

'Yes,' said Lady Slane, 'but more people are really of the same mind than you would believe. They take a great deal of trouble to conceal it, and only a crisis calls it out. For instance, if you were to die,' – but what she really meant was, If I were to die – 'I daresay you would find that your grandfather had understood you (me) better than you (I) think.'

'That's mere sentimentality,' said Deborah firmly; 'naturally, death startles everybody, even grandfather and great-aunt Carrie – it reminds them of the things they prefer to ignore. My point about the people I like, is not that they dwell morbidly on death, but that they keep continually a sense of what, to them, matters in life. Death, after all, is an incident. Life is an incident too. The thing I mean lies outside both. And it doesn't seem compatible with the sort of life grandfather and great-aunt Carrie think I ought to lead. Am I wrong, or are they?'

Lady Slane perceived one last opportunity for annoying Herbert and Carrie. Let them call her a wicked old woman! she knew that she was no such thing. The child was an artist, and must have her way. There were other people in plenty to carry on the work of the world, to earn and enjoy its rewards, to suffer its malice and return its wounds in kind; the small and rare fraternity to which Deborah belonged, indifferent to gilded lures, should be free to go obscurely but ardently about its business. In the long run, with the strange bedlam always in process of sorting itself out, as the present-day became history, the poets and the prophets counted for more than the conquerors. Christ himself was of their company.

She could form no estimate of Deborah's talents; that was beside the point. Achievement was good, but the spirit was better. To reckon by achievements was to make a concession to the prevailing system of the world; it was a departure from the austere, disinterested, exacting standards that Lady Slane and her kindred recognised. Yet what she said was not at all in accordance with her thoughts; she said, 'Oh dear, if I hadn't given away that fortune I could have made you independent.'

Deborah laughed. She wanted advice, she said, not money. Lady Slane knew very well that she did not really want advice either; she wanted only to be strengthened and supported in her resolution. Very well, if she wanted approval, she should have it. 'Of course you are right, my dear,' she said quietly.

They talked for a while longer, but Deborah, feeling herself folded into peace and sympathy, noticed that her great-grandmother's mind wandered a little into some maze of confusion to which Deborah held no guiding thread. It was natural at Lady Slane's age. At moments she appeared to be talking about herself, then recalled her wits, and with pathetic clumsiness tried to cover up the slip, rousing herself to speak eagerly of the girl's future, not of some event which had gone wrong in the distant past. Deborah was too profoundly lulled and happy to wonder much what that event could be. This hour of union with the old woman soothed her like music, like chords lightly touched in the evening, with the shadows closing and the moths bruising beyond an open window. She leaned against the old woman's knee as a support, a prop, drowned, enfolded, in warmth, dimness, and soft harmonious sounds. The hurly-burly receded; the clangour was stilled; her grandfather and her great-aunt Carrie lost their angular importance and shrivelled to little gesticulating puppets with parchment faces and silly wavering hands; other values rose up like great archangels in the room, and towered and spread their wings. Inexplicable associations floated into Deborah's mind; she remembered how once she had seen a young woman in a white dress leading a white borzoi across the darkness of a southern port. This physical and mental contact with her great-grandmother – so far removed in years, so closely attuned in spirit – stripped off the coverings from the small treasure of short experience that she had jealously stored away. She caught herself wondering whether she could afterwards recapture the incantation of this hour sufficiently to render it into terms of music. Her desire to render an experience in terms of music transcended even her interest in her great-grandmother as a human being; a form of egoism which she knew her great-grandmother would neither resent nor misunderstand. The impulse which had led her to her great-grandmother was a right impulse. The sense of enveloping music proved that. On some remote piano the chords were struck, and they were chords which had no meaning, no existence, in the world inhabited by her grandfather and her great-aunt Carrie; but in her great-grandmother's world they had their value and their significance. But she must not tire her great-grandmother, thought Deborah, suddenly realising that the old voice had ceased its maunderings and that the spell of an hour was broken. Her great-grandmother was asleep. Her chin had fallen forward on to the laces at her breast. Her lovely hands were limp in their repose. As Deborah rose silently, and silently let herself out into the street, being careful not to slam the door behind her, the chords of her imagination died away.

Genoux, bringing in the tray an hour later, announcing

'Miladi est servie,' altered her formula to a sudden, 'Mon Dieu, mais qu'est-ce que c'est ça – Miladi est morte.'

'It was to be expected,' said Carrie, mopping her eyes as she had not mopped them over the death of her father; 'it was to be expected, Mr Bucktrout. Yet it comes as a shock. My poor mother was such a very exceptional woman, as you know – though I'm sure I don't see how you should have known it, for she was, of course, only your tenant. A correspondent in *The Times* described her this morning as a rare spirit. Just what I always said myself: a rare spirit.' Carrie had forgotten the many other things she had said. 'A little difficult to manage some-times,' she added, stung by a sudden thought of FitzGeorge's fortune; 'unpractical to a degree, but practical things are not the only things that count, are they, Mr Bucktrout?' *The Times* had said that too. 'My poor mother had a beautiful nature. I don't say that I should always have acted myself as she some-times acted. Her motives were sometimes a little difficult to follow. Quixotic, you know, and – shall we say? – injudicious. Besides, she could be very stubborn. There were times when she wouldn't be guided, which was unfortunate, considering how unpractical she was. We should all be in a very different position now had she been willing to listen to us. However, it's no good crying over spilt milk, is it?' said Carrie, giving Mr Bucktrout what was meant to be a brave smile.

Mr Bucktrout made no answer. He disliked Carrie. He won-dered how anyone so hard and so hypocritical could be the daughter of someone so sensitive and so honest as his old friend. He was determined to reveal to Carrie by no word or look how deeply he felt the loss of Lady Slane.

'There is a man downstairs who can take the measurements for the coffin, should you wish,' he said.

Carrie stared. So they had been right about this Mr

Bucktrout: a heartless old man, lacking the decency to find one suitable phrase about poor Mother; Carrie herself had been generous enough to repeat those words about the rare spirit; really, on the whole, she considered her little oration over her mother to be a very generous tribute, when one remembered the tricks her mother had played on them all. She had felt extremely righteous as she pronounced it, and according to her code Mr Bucktrout ought to have said something graceful in reply. No doubt he had expected to pull some plums out of the pudding himself, and had been embittered by his failure. The thought of the old shark's discomfiture was Carrie's great consolation. Mr Bucktrout was just the sort of man who tried to hook an unsuspecting old lady. And now, full of revengefulness, he fell back on bringing a man to make the coffin.

'My brother, Lord Slane, will be here shortly to make all the necessary arrangements,' she replied haughtily.

Mr Gosheron, however, was already at the door. He came in tilting his bowler hat, but whether he tilted it towards the silent presence of Lady Slane in her bed, or towards Carrie standing at the foot, was questionable. Mr Gosheron in his capacity as an undertaker was well accustomed to death; still, his feeling for Lady Slane had always been much warmer than for a mere client. He had already tried to give some private expression to his emotion by determining to sacrifice his most treasured piece of wood as the lid for her coffin.

'Her ladyship makes a lovely corpse,' he said to Mr Bucktrout.

They both ignored Carrie.

'Lovely in life, lovely in death, is what I always say,' said Mr Gosheron. 'It's astonishing, the beauty that death brings out. My old grandfather told me that, who was in the same line of business, and for fifty years I've watched to see if his words were true. 'Beauty in life,' he used to say, 'may come from good

172

dressing and what-not, but for beauty in death you have to fall back on character.' Now look at her ladyship, Mr Bucktrout. Is it true, or isn't it? To tell you the truth,' he added confidentially, 'if I want to size a person up, I look at them and picture them dead. That always gives it away, especially as they don't know you're doing it. The first time I ever set eyes on her ladyship, I said, yes, she'll do; and now that I see her as I pictured her then I still say it. She wasn't never but half in this world, anyhow.'

'No, she wasn't,' said Mr Bucktrout, who, now that Mr Gosheron had arrived, was willing to talk about Lady Slane, 'and she never came to terms with it either. She had the best that it could give her – all the things she didn't want. She considered the lilies of the field, Mr Gosheron.'

'She did, Mr Bucktrout; many a phrase out of the Bible have I applied to her ladyship. But people will stand things in the Bible that they won't stand in common life. They don't seem to see the sense of it when they meet it in their own homes, although they'll put on a reverent face when they hear it read out from a lectern.'

Oh goodness, thought Carrie, will these two old men never stop talking across Mother like a Greek chorus? She had arrived at Hampstead in a determined frame of mind: she would be generous, she would be forgiving – and some genuine emotion had come to her aid – but now her self-possession cracked and her ill-temper and grievances came boiling up. This agent and this undertaker, who talked so securely and so sagaciously, what could they know of her mother?

'Perhaps,' she snapped, 'you had better leave my mother's funeral oration to be pronounced by one of her own family.'

Mr Bucktrout and Mr Gosheron both turned gravely towards her. She saw them suddenly as detached figures; figures of fun certainly, yet also figures of justice. Their eyes stripped away the protection of her decent hypocrisy. She felt that they judged her; that Mr Gosheron, according to his use and principle, was imagining her as a corpse; was narrowing his eyes to help the effort of his imagination; was laying her out upon a bed, examining her without the defences she could no longer control. That phrase about the rare spirit shrivelled to a cinder. Mr Bucktrout and Mr Gosheron were in league with her mother, and no phrases could cover up the truth from such an alliance.

'In the presence of death,' she said to Mr Gosheron, taking refuge in a last convention, 'you might at least take off your hat.'

THE EDWARDIANS

Vita Sackville-West

Introduced by Juliet Nicolson

'As opulent and ambiguous as the author herself'
Victoria Glendinning

'He had climbed on to the roof not only because for years such
exercise had been his favourite pastime but because it was now his
only certain method of escape. Escape was a necessity; otherwise,
his mother expected him to play the host . . . he went up an angle
of the sloping tiles, to sit astride the peak of the roof; tore his shirt
open, fanned his flushed face, and drank the air in large draughts.
A cloud of white pigeons wheeled above him in the sky.
Acres of red-brown roof surrounded him, heraldic beasts
carved in stone sitting at each corner of the gables.'

At nineteen, Sebastian is a duke and heir to the vast country
estate, Chevron. A deep sense of tradition binds him to his
inheritance, though he loathes the social circus he is a part of.
Deception, infidelity and greed hide beneath the glittering surface
of good manners. Among the guests at a lavish party are two
people who will change Sebastian's life: Lady Roehampton, a great
beauty who will initiate Sebastian in the art of love; and Leonard
Anquetil, a polar explorer who sees Sebastian as condemned by
his inheritance. Anquetil's subversive influence leads Sebastian
and his free-spirited sister Viola to question their destiny.

A portrait of fashionable society at the height of the era,
The Edwardians revealed all that was glamorous about the period –
and all that was to lead to its downfall. First published in 1930,
it was Vita Sackville West's most successful book, selling
twenty thousand copies in two months.

NO SIGNPOSTS IN THE SEA

Vita Sackville-West

Introduced by Victoria Glendinning

Published the year before her death, this haunting,
elegiac tale is Vita Sackville-West's final novel.

Edmund Carr is at sea in more ways than one. An eminent
journalist and self-made man, he has recently discovered that
he has only a short time to live. Leaving his job on a Fleet Street
paper, he takes a passage on a cruise ship where he knows
that Laura, a beautiful and intelligent widow whom
he secretly admires, will be a fellow passenger.

Exhilarated by the distant vista of exotic islands never to be
visited and his conversations with Laura, Edmund finds himself
rethinking all his values. A voyage on many levels, those long
purposeless days at sea find Edmund relinquishing the past
as he discovers the joys and the pain of a love he is
simultaneously determined to conceal.

'A moving and original book . . . her final testament'
Victoria Glendinning

virago

To buy any of our books and to find out more
about Virago Press and Virago Modern Classics,
our authors and titles, as well as events and
book club forum, visit our websites

www.virago.co.uk
www.littlebrown.co.uk

and follow us on Twitter

@ViragoBooks

To order any Virago titles p & p free in the UK,
please contact our mail order supplier on:

+ 44 (0)1832 737525

Customers not based in the UK should contact
the same number for appropriate postage
and packing costs.